Kenkey for EWES

& OTHER VERY SHORT STORIES

AAD Asiedu I DH Dzah I JJ Johnson (Editors)

DAkpabli

DAKPABLI & ASSOCIATES
ACCRA

ISBN: 978-9988-2-8553-1

ABAVANNA SERIES (AV5)

Edited by James Anquandah (j.anquandah@yahoo.com)
Original Cover Art: David Tamsey instagram.com/davidtamsey

Cover design and Book Layout by multiPIXEL Limited
P O Box DC 1965, Dansoman, Accra, Ghana
Email: multipixelmails@gmail.com
Tel: +233 302 333 502 | +233 246 725 060 | +233 246 210 862

Published by
Dakpabli & Associates
P O Box 7465, Accra North, Accra, Ghana
Tel: +233 264 339 066 | +233 244 704 250 | +233 247 896 375
Email: info@dakpabli.com

Contents

Editors' Note

A couple of years ago, the FlashFictionGhana Team thought it would be a great idea to experiment with an anthology of Ghanaian flash fiction. The products of this experiment, conducted together with twenty-seven Ghanaian writers, are contained in this book. At the start of the project, we were glad to see writers depart from more predictable and conventional comical and love stories to explore the paranormal and mysterious while keeping a finger on the pulse of contemporary Ghanaian society.

This anthology contains 25 new stories, and 25 'old' stories, which we consider to be some of the best published on the flashfictionghana.com blog. Thus, this anthology is in many ways a natural outgrowth of the work already being done on the blog. These stories carry the spirit with which FlashFictionGhana was born; to use this convenient genre as a way of bringing to life the Ghanaian experience in all its varied facets.

These stories represent the budding creative spirit of the current generation of young Ghanaian writers. These new voices have become the refreshing perspective from which to consider the Ghanaian narrative in a thousand or less words.

Happy reading,

The FlashFictionGhana Team
(Adelaide, Daniel, and Jesse)

Cooking with Mama

Abena Karikari

"Ei, is that how you're slicing the onions?" Mama asks.

Pause.

"Yes, that's how I've been slicing them. Why?" I respond.

Mama shrugs. "Ah well. I guess that's ok."

Longer pause.

"How do you want me to slice them?" I give in and ask.

Mama's smile is eager. "Give me the knife and let me show you."

I stifle an exasperated sigh and hand over the knife.

Mama starts cutting up the onions thinly. "You see, this is how

I've always done it, just how your father likes it."

I roll my eyes. Thankfully, Mama doesn't see.

"Ok, now start heating up the saucepan. We'll pour in the palm oil in a bit."

I turn on the gas cooker and place the saucepan on a medium flame.

"Is everything else ready for the stew?" Mama asks as she finishes slicing the last onion.

I mentally check off the items needed for the stew as my eyes sweep the kitchen counter: *Palm oil, chopped up tomatoes, agushi already blended, powdered shrimps, opened can of tomato paste, salt, pepper…what's left?*

"Where's the smoked fish?" Mama interrupts my mental run through.

Aha! That's what was missing! I run into the storeroom and grab one medium sized fish from the basket we keep all smoked fish. The beady eye of the lifeless fish stares at me. "Sorry." I whisper a futile apology.

"Aba, stop talking to the fish; it's already dead. Bring it," Mama says, without even turning around. That woman's sense of hearing is eerily good for her age.

"Break up the fish into smaller pieces and make sure you take out all the bones", she instructs.

I roll my eyes. "Yes Mama."

"Aba, who are you talking to in there?" Papa calls from the living room.

"Nobody!" I yell back. I glance at Mama.

She smiles at me and pours palm oil into the heated pan. Soon, the almost cloying smell fills the kitchen.

After I'm done with the smoked fish, I peel and cut up the plantain to boil while Mama prepares the Kontomire stew. After some thirty minutes, the stew is ready and the boiled plantain, which finished cooking earlier, sits in a food flask waiting. Mama dishes out the food onto plates and places them on a tray.

"Take it to your father; I can hear his stomach growling from here."

I laugh. I pick up the tray laden with a plate each of boiled plantains and the Kontomire stew we've just cooked together and head out of the kitchen. At the door, I turn to look at my mother.

"He misses you, Mama," I say softly.

Mama looks sad for a moment. "I know. I miss him too." She smiles again. "But he has you, so I know he'll be fine. You will both be fine."

I nod, encouraged by Mama's confidence in me.

I go into the living room and place the tray carefully on the coffee table in front of Papa. I return to the kitchen and fill a bowl with water for him to wash his hands. I grab a napkin on my way back to the living room and note vaguely that Mama is no longer in the kitchen.

"Medaase." Papa thanks me. He washes his hands and dries them with the napkin. I look on as Papa breaks off a piece of plantain, scoops up some of the Kontomire stew and pops it into his mouth. His eyes widen as he chews. For a moment, I feel myself start to panic. *Is there something wrong with the stew? A stray fish bone maybe?*

"Papa, is something wrong?" I ask. While Mama was alive he ate only food cooked by her, so I have every reason to be anxious.

"Aba, this tastes exactly like your mother used to make it!" He exclaims in wonder. A look of nostalgia crosses his face as he shakes his head and returns to his food.

I turn away so he doesn't see the tear that comes to my eye. Before the tear falls, I feel a slight breeze on my arm and I smell a waft of the flowery perfume my mother used to wear. I smile; Mama is still with us.

A Minute's Silence

Adelaide Awo Darkoa Asiedu

We sit. Afraid to sigh or even to breathe too loudly; these sixty seconds hold our collective breath. I look at her face - closely. Every tint to its colouration interests me, every pore of her skin. Her face is drooping. The mouth droops, an upturned, squished horseshoe. Her eyes droop, uneven, overturned almonds. Even her tears seem to droop; half-moons instead of whatever shape tears are expected to be. And then they glide down her face, tiny rivulets.

I did not know her father—only that he died, hence, her droopiness. I do not know her father. Yet in these sixty seconds, I, like the others, am silent.

I wonder why we are. I wondered why last year, when Nana's mother passed. And in church, the year before that, I did not quite understand why we stood mum for a full one minute for the sake of the late great Bishop Boye. I have no doubt that in the future I will wonder again. What use have the dead for our sixty seconds? Will our silence somehow revive them? Or, when we release the breaths these sixty seconds have held, will they find their way up her father's nostrils and remedy her stubborn droopiness?

I imagine that she must be thinking of her father. Sixty seconds will not be enough. I however, have no thoughts of him upon which to chew, so they stretch on. My jaws find the silence most disagreeable and cannot wait to ejaculate some word to mask the degree of irreverence taking place in my head. It strikes me that perhaps my head is not the only one guilty of irreverence.

I have strong doubts that the woman over there with the infant in a red shirt strapped to her front is thinking things anywhere near the subject of the deceased father. The toddler, unconcerned in the baby carrier, keeps her eyes shut in sleep.

I can bet that the child eyeing that stick of kebab poking out of the rubber bag in his father's hand is not meditating on the sorrows flowing from the loss of one's father. The teenage girl to my right clutching her phone most likely cannot wait to check her WhatsApp messages. And that old man with his head bowed, well, he just may be considering the beloved deceased, seeing that his turn to be remembered may well be soon. But his appearance is much too plain, too boring for my mind's contemplation.

I look outside the window. The moon still glows. The breeze still plays with the leaves on the trees. Nature itself is guilty…

I look at *her*, not just her face. Her shoulders, as you would expect, sag. But her arms, thank heavens, are folded in front of her. They appear, quite appropriately, to be embracing each other. And her legs, they tremble a bit, though I can hardly tell beneath the sombre darkness of her ankle-length skirt.

She appears very affected by our fifty seconds so far, while the rest of us, with the exception of the odd friend, gently patting the sagging shoulder, and the other standing behind her, in subdued solidarity, obviously are not. All of us, observing a minute's silence for a man we never even knew existed. We are giving a dead man sixty seconds of our lives, for which he has no use, with a topping of irreverence. We are – never mind what we are doing, the sixty seconds are up now, as they ought to be!

The man behind the mic states the obvious. Then she, the bereaved, moves towards the mic, legs still trembling. She mouths an almost inaudible "thank you". Her lips change from drooping fixtures to a tentative, sad, smile.

It's odd isn't it, that a minute's silence should produce a smile?

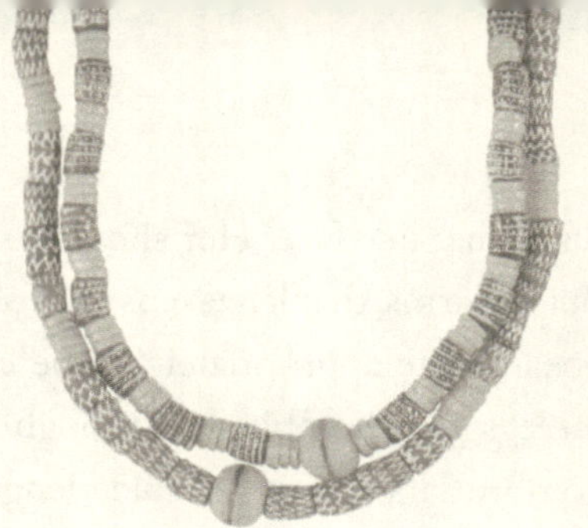

Red Means Stop

Adelaide Awo Darkoa Asiedu

The dress is red. Tight. Actually, it's more than tight, its seams cling to my body. Its red and my brown could easily be the same fabric, but my brown is skin and the red is my dress. Somewhere in between my thigh and my knee, the red gives way once more to my brown. In truth, the mirror reflects more brown than red; perfect. My clock says it's time to go, and so I do. Through the window, down one ledge, each leg navigates its way to the grass below. The wall is a walk over, literally. Nobody sees me, except the night. I have no fears. The night may be your foe, but it is my ally, my element. Ma is sleeping, for sure. Da is at work. They do not see me. They never do. Accra is calling. I do not look back.

The light is red. I mean the small one blinking at the base of my laptop. My battery is low. I grab the charger and plug it in to the power source quickly. The light changes from red to green, lighting up my screen, as well as my face, with a smile. "Hello".

The message pops up from my inbox. "Thought I had lost you there for a minute. We must get back to where we were." Considering where we were, I should be horrified by this proposition. I should be indignant and insulted. I am nothing but capitulating. I know I am married but…it's been hopeless from the start. My husband is a broken record and I am tired of trying to fix things. We get back to where we were. As usual, letters on a screen are no longer enough. We quickly switch from Email to Skype. I wonder why we constantly repeat this ritual. Maybe it's because we've never actually met in person; our only link, our clicks on the internet. Maybe it's because we are thousands of miles apart, oceans actually. Accra is a dot on the map compared to where he is. Or perhaps it's because we started that way. If anyone knows about little drops of water, I do. I should be mortified. I should want to see the light go red. But I am not and I do not. I make sure the cable is firmly plugged in. But it's alright. Nobody sees me. No one ever does. The lights are off in my room. The young lady down the hall must think I am sleeping. The husband is working late. I am doing some work of my own, the personal kind.

The ink on the sign board is red. "Verna's Place" it says. I am familiar with the sign board. I am familiar with this place. I am even more familiar with Verna and her girls. She says the one she has for me tonight is one of her best. Now that I am a "premium member" of her less than respectable "establishment", I have access to "the best". Work ended a while ago. But nobody knows that, and they never will. After all, this too is a business of sorts. The two women at home must be sound asleep. Sleep, blessed sleep; my only respite from their constant yapping about wanting this and that, and about how I am an absent husband/father. Verna leads me upstairs. This is my first time upstairs. I have always only been downstairs. I look forward to what awaits me. We stop at a door. There's a picture stuck to it. It shows me the backside of the luscious configuration of brown curves that awaits me behind the door. The picture looks vaguely familiar, but only vaguely. Verna smiles, wide. Of course, she does. Each upstairs door she opens is another GH¢1000 in her bank account. She leaves. I can handle things from here. As the door creaks open, I peek in, expectant. Her head is lowered. I see brown in a red dress. She lifts her eyes seductively. They stay glued to my face and widen as the mouth breaks into a twisted O. The question hangs in the air like a two-way bomb, "Daddy?!"

The Rustling of the Leaves

Adelaide Awo Darkoa Asiedu

She stared up into the sky for the millionth time that day. Well, probably not into the sky, but into the bright gold spots of light that seeped through the canopy of dark green mango leaves. The sun's rays painted dancing patterns against the background of leaves swaying in the breeze. She felt a bit like them, these leaves that moved not of their own accord, but simply swished wherever the wind blew. Occasionally, one would fall gently to the ground, another addition to the graveyard of varying degrees of rotting leaves lying beneath her feet.

She wondered, if the leaves had voices, would they cry out when they fell? Would they resist the call of the wind or simply mouth their contentment, in humble submission to their fate? Maybe the rustling sounds they made were whispers housing the secret desires of rebel leaves, who like her, yearned for something greater than kowtowing to some unseen, all-powerful wind, but could see no way of escape, other than the piles of decaying foliage beneath. The life of the leaf; dance to the tune of the wind, or shrivel up and die…. had become her life…

Looking down at the ground now, she traced another seemingly meaningless image in the sand with her big toe. It was a shapeless, almost hideous creation, nothing like the strokes of her paint brush against canvas. There was life in her brush and it gave her paintings breath so that they would leap out of their frames, giving some silent message to whoever cared to look. Their yellows spoke of happiness and their reds of anger and their blues of a myriad of things that could only be decoded by the discerning eye. Right now, her toe carried the opposite of the blood that coursed through her brush and her sand monster spoke of death; the death of the leaves and the death of her dreams.

She stood up. Enough time had already been wasted under the mango trees- not as if there was anything important to be done at the moment. She was playing a waiting game and her time was almost up. She had merely hours left before being shipped out to be made an engineer. What manner of engineer she would be, she could not fathom. But her father was the wind and she was the leaf and her available options were to bend or fall. She was born into an already planned out life. Father had said, "Awura will go to kindergarten early" and of course she did. "Awura will be the best pupil in her primary school", and she had obligingly worked hard at that. "Awura will get into the best high school in the country" and she had all but killed herself to do so and had done so. She had lived to please her father. She had basked in the glow of his attention and flourished under his praise. But over the sunshine of his approval always hovered the cloud of her art.

She would never forget her first scribbles with a crayon in the kindergarten. She had started schooling at one and half years instead of the two and half. The colours had made her almost giddy with excitement and she had discovered from that moment that she had been imbued with the power to turn colour into spirit and that her markings on any surface, were not just ordinary, but spoke volumes. That was the birth of the cloud.

She had bent, oh how she had bent and been blown and tossed by his stone will and steely resolve to mould her into the lead character of the script he had written even before she was born; an answer to the questions raised by his unfulfilled dreams. She had played the part well but it had been consistently adulterated by the additional lines sparked by her fire. And her father would have none of that. So, for years she had painted in secret so that his conditional sunshine would never give way to a night that gave no guarantees of a moon's guiding light.

But now the time had come when she was no longer a tender green leaf, desperate to drink in the sun's radiance. She was dark green like the mango leaves above her head, but unlike them, she had a mouth and a will and a fire that gnawed at the seams of her soul, urging her to do more than just rustle.

So, she got up and went into the house. She went to the file cabinet beneath the staircase and gathered them. There were some beneath her bed and she gathered them too. The sack in the basement was full of them and she gathered them also. There were piles of them in the store room that her father never entered and she gathered them from there too. Then she picked up the last ones from her late mother's locked up art gallery, whose key she kept in the locket hung around her neck.

She walked to her father's study and entered before he could answer her knocks. She told him she was tired and could not star in the charade anymore adding that she was a time bomb about to explode for which reason she would not be made into an engineer. And *he* sat there and exploded but she stood firm and would not be blasted to bits by his dynamite. In response to his tirade, she spoke no words but would pick them up one by one. First, the painting of the happy family she had made the year before her mother had parted; the painting where the sun was a bright yellow and the sky a true blue and their smiles were more than bared teeth. Then, the one from her thirteenth birthday, that depicted running blood and a broken heart, when her mother's death snuffed out her father's joy and grew the cloud between her husband and their daughter. Then she showed him the black hole swallowing the colours which carried her creativity. And then she picked up the shimmering gold work of art that her mother had painted for her just before the cancer had stolen her, in whose centre, she had carved in the words, "Follow your dreams, then you will shine, my star". Those words were like lyrics to the song of her heart beat. But her father was a tone-deaf bomb that refused to be deactivated. She would not remain to be torn into little pieces as he detonated, she would rather evacuate.

So, she turned around with the gold painting in her arms and her admission letter to the art school somewhere in Paris, which he had refused to look at, and walked, away from her rustling, up the path of her dreams, so she could shine. Before she stepped out of the compound, packed up to be made into a star, she cast a sidelong glance at the leaves of the mango trees and whispered a parting message to them, "I'm sorry my old friends, but I had to do more than rustle to the wind". And then she flew…

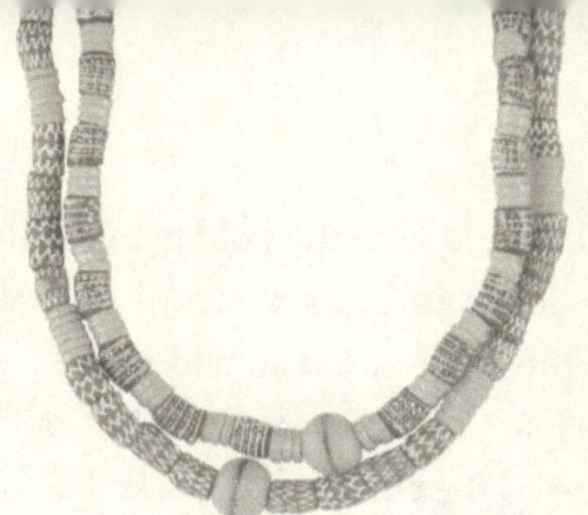

5840

Akua Serwaa Amankwah

Today, one of those evenings the skies are on the verge of rain; the kind of gloomy weather that matches my mood.

May 2014
09.58pm

My hands are trembling as I touch your skin. Your breathing, as usual, is irregular and your eyes firmly shut. You have such beautiful eyelashes. They are long and thick and exactly what every woman needs to use mascara on. They're wasted on you. Your nose, oh that bulbous nose. It hasn't shrunk one bit. I touch it, hopefully expecting you to move just a little. But you don't. I wish you'd surprise everyone and just open your eyes. Just once, just for me. Tell me this was all a joke. Kiss me senseless, allow me to insult you, then we go back to normal. But no, the complex little machines, the ventilator, they are all reminders that nothing is normal.

I begged the nurse not to come around this evening. Tonight is just for you and me.

I sit at the edge of the uncomfortable hospital bed. With difficulty, I wiggle up beside you. I won't cry today, I promise myself. I will not cry. I won't cry. I won't cry. I will not—

Salty, hot, painful, gut-wrenching tears trickle down my face.

I try to dab at my eyes with a handkerchief.

I trace little kisses on your face, your neck, your chest. I wonder what you're thinking, wherever you are. Do you know your wife is here, kissing you? Do you feel my warm, trembling hands? Do you feel my heart thumping so loudly I fear it would jump out of my chest and run out of these cold, grey doors?

Do you remember tomorrow is our 16th anniversary?

Then I envelope you in my arms and close my eyes to happier times. Times when you were alive.

A beautiful kind of weather; one that sets the tone for a lifelong romance.

One that sets the tone for love. *Better.*

I remember the first day I saw you. I'd attended a party with my big sister. I wasn't even sure why I went; my sister was the social butterfly and I a wallflower. I didn't know anyone, and I made no effort to socialize. I found some corner to sit, and later when I was getting up to go for some juice, I realized my skirt had been ripped by a nail shabbily hammered on the chair. I tried to get up, and realized the rip was bigger than I'd thought. My eyes darted around to see if anyone had noticed me. Then I turned around nervously, and your eyes caught mine. Your expression was a mixture of amusement and pity. You came to my aid anyway. You helped me cover my torn skirt with your cardigan, and then you got me another skirt. It was short and tight and uncomfortable and so I ended up still using your cardigan to cover my demure self.

Then we talked and bonded over countless bottles of Maltina and chargrilled Suya pork. I don't really remember what you said, because I kept looking at your lips and then your lovely eyes framed by your eyelashes. Then, so you could see me again you asked me to keep your cardigan. I smiled. I had been waiting for you to say that all night.

My sister was shocked I'd met someone, and when she saw you she whispered to me. "Wow, such a nice guy. But that nose, sister. The nose has a life of its own". Then we giggled and nicknamed you "Big Nose". And later my sister would be the middle woman, exchanging love letters love notes and arranging meetings for us.

Then just a little over a year later, you came home to ask for my hand in marriage, and everyone told you how lucky you were, because I was lovely and definitely STD-free (they said this because one of your friends came from honeymoon with a painful little present; gonorrhea from his wife.)

A Case of Cravings and A Baby with Ding Dongs.

April 2000
8.22am

You wouldn't leave me alone when I got pregnant with our first child. You said my breasts had become huge and you wanted to touch them all the time. I was still smitten with you. You had a great sense of humour, and you loved to tease me especially because of my cravings. At dawn, I would torture you to go get Dede's soft, billowy loaves of honey buttermilk bread because they were most delicious when fresh out of the oven. I'm sure when my little one tumbled into the world you heaved a huge sigh of relief. And oh, the birth! The doctor first thought it was a girl when it came. Then you shrieked. "My daughter's got two little ding dongs?!", and we realized it was a boy. But we called you *Daddy Ding Dong* till Kofi turned three.

Mama and Baby, Angels Moving to a Better Country

You were the first one they told when my mother died. You came home that night, and you pampered me and fed me and you cradled me in your arms. And then you said it so softly I thought I'd imagined it. *Mama T has passed on.* And you were there every single moment when I suffered nightmares. You handled my mood swings, my unexpected tears, and my unexplained bouts of sadness; because you knew how close I was to my mother.

You consoled me when I had that miscarriage. It would have been a girl. Then you told me you would be my little girl, and that day you wore one of my dresses and pranced about, bright pink barrettes in your hair, and you made me and the boys laugh and laugh.

Of Christmas and carols and too much food and too much everything.

And of you hovering between this earth and that better country.

December 2011

You'd travelled and you'd promised me you'd be home in time for Christmas. I pushed you. I should have asked you to wait when you complained you were tired. Yet I spurred you on, telling you I'd made your special jollof with grilled chicken. And you drove for six hours straight without rest, and you slept behind the wheel. You didn't even see the oncoming truck. And you have not woken up till now.

A Support System now on Life Support: A complete and Irrevocable Irony of my Life.

May 2014
5.40am

The doctors have put you in an induced coma, and you've been on life support for nearly a month now. They say you might not make it. They have said so many things which have broken my heart.

They will take you off life support this morning.

I sleep in fits and starts. Every time I open my eyes, I look at you, and I cry. You're leaving me on our anniversary. Today, I have loved you for 5,840 days. I have loved you since I saw you at that party. I love you still. I kiss you for the umpteenth time, and I whisper 'Goodbye, my love, my tuntum broni, my everything. Tell Mama T I said hello. Take good care of our baby that was too perfect for this earth.'

It's too early for the sun to be shining this brightly. When I move out it blinds my eyes and disrupts my tears.

May 2014
6.30am

I'm at the morgue when one of your nurses rushes there. "Mrs, come with me please". She's panting. There is no time to ask questions. When I get to your room what catches my eye is the EKG, where just an hour ago there'd been a flat line. Now, there is a tiny movement, and then a peak is slowly beginning to draw a pattern. My heart starts beating, and I rush to your bedside.

There you are, you magnificent idiot, and your eyelids are fluttering.

Cake

Akua Serwaa Amankwah

The alarm clock's devilish shrill yanks me from a beautiful dream. 3am. I have to bake her birthday cake before she goes to school. As always, my heart starts beating furiously as I turn to my left to look at my baby. She's breathing. I sigh in relief. She's an angel, sleeping peacefully. I lean toward her, and I kiss her forehead. "Happy Birthday", I whisper. She smiles a little but doesn't wake up. She's devastatingly beautiful. She's smart. She's clingy. I love that. She's all over her mother. *Mother.* Every time she says that word I try not to wince.

I smile and ruffle her nappy hair. Her hair, which her silly school authorities want me to cut because braided hair is not accepted. Idiots. No one is cutting my baby's hair!

I am still staring at her. Adorableness oozes from her. She's bubbly and sweet and full of joy and thinks no one will do harm to her, that everyone loves her. They tell me I have a beautiful daughter. That comment is usually accompanied by a look of surprise. How does an average looking baker have such a beautiful daughter? I try to smile. But I'm pained.

I love her Cupid bow mouth and the way she scowls when she's hungry. I love the way her face crumples when she's sad, or her forlorn expression when she tells me about her bad day at school. I love her spontaneous giggles, and her hugs from behind, her pudgy hands claiming my skirts.

I call her Cake because she loves it so much. She's a sucker for my moist banana cake. And especially on her birthday today, I have to bake a large chocolate cake for her to share with her friends at school. I drag myself out of bed and trudge to the kitchen.

I preheat the oven even before I sit down to mix the ingredients. I am always happy on her birthday. But I also get jumpy and so many emotions flood me. I get to work. It's easy for me. I've done this a thousand times. And yet, my hands are trembling. My heart suddenly beats a bit too fast. I stop. I sit down for a while. And against my wishes, I relive that night.

It was my friend Adiba's idea. She was a fancy nurse at a fancy hospital. She told me to give birth there, she could tell the workers I was her sister, and that would slash three-quarters of the fee I would pay. Even the remaining quarter was expensive. I didn't want to at first. The Victoria Hospital was too posh, too beautiful for me. Yet, that day when my water broke, I found myself being wheeled inside their plush rooms, Adiba by my side.

That day I was too sick to know what was going on. I knew something was wrong, because the doctor kept on asking questions as I wove in and out of consciousness. Why hadn't I been coming for constant check-ups? Was I really Adiba's sister? I didn't understand the medical terms; I just knew something was wrong.

The doctor decided on a caesarean section at the last minute, and I don't remember much; I blacked out. They tried to wake me up several times, but I was too weak to respond, I was told later. When I finally opened my eyes, it was midnight, and most of the nurses had left. I struggled to get out of my bed, and I realized my baby was not with me. I made it to the nursery. I had to see my baby. One of the nurses saw me and waved at me. She showed me where my baby was. "It's a girl", she gushed, smiling. I smiled, but my heart jumped. My baby. She wasn't breathing well.

I went back to the nursery several times. Each time, I realized that my baby might not even last till morning, but the nurses were too busy chit chatting to go on ward-rounds.

At three am, I went back to the nursery. I picked my little one up. Her breathing was faint now. I acted without thinking. I looked at the next baby, and I picked it up. It looked like my little one and it was fast asleep. I switched them seamlessly, and swapped the name cards on their tiny hands. When I looked up, the two nurses who'd been sleeping when I got there were still snoring. I went back to my bed. I slept poorly because I thought one of the nurses would come up to me, and shake me awake to tell me, *I saw what you did*. But it never happened.

The next morning, I asked to go home, even though I wasn't fully recovered. I was afraid I'd be found out. Adiba pulled some strings, and convinced the doctor to let me go, and when she came to see me later that day, she told me about the sad incident of how one of the new mothers had lost their babies. "You're so lucky", Adiba told me, a sad smile on her face, and I wanted to cry and admit it to her. But no. I didn't want a dead baby. I hadn't suffered nine months in vain. I nodded.

I never met that mother, but I wonder where she is now. Would she ever imagine she took the wrong one home? The dead one? Would she think she buried another baby? Would she know that somewhere in a small neighbourhood, a baker was raising her beautiful one?

But now it scares me how she looks so different; so unlike me, so unlike her father. When Cake calls me mother, I jump.

My hands dusted with flour, I make my way to the bedroom. She still sleeps peacefully. I smile a little. In a couple of hours, she'll be up. She has no idea that six years ago today, she was swapped. I walk back to the kitchen, and feel my guilt hanging over me like an invisible cloak. I pick up my phone impulsively, my heart beating faster. I have to tell someone. I dial the first number that comes into my head. It's just 4am now. Adiba's voice is groggy, laced with sleep. "Hallo?" is the word that comes out. "Adiba, I have to tell you something…," I start, and I begin to cry.

Purgatory

Akua Serwaa Amankwah

They argued again. Painful streams of invective flew back and forth in their bedroom. Anike's words knew no boundaries; they touched on the sacred, they pricked and attacked Adjoka. They both yelled. His black eyes were fire in the dark. Unbridled rage seeped through her whole being.

She pushed past him and opened her wardrobe. There was no way she was spending the night with this mad man. She took her lingerie and a few other things she would need for the guest room.

Time had been cruel to their marriage. Only six years ago, they had been inseparable, incredibly loved up, newlyweds. The fun they had had; skinny dipping in their small pool every evening, talking for hours on end, murmuring endearments to each other every now and then. Those had been good times.

But something snapped along the way. The knot they had tied loosened up. He began giving other women attention. She did the same to make him jealous. But then, she began to like one new 'friend' a little bit too much. Sai was unlike any man she'd ever met. He was younger than she was. He was spontaneous, silly, sexy, and he spoiled her rotten. Sai made her happy. Adjoka made her depressed.

This new argument started when Adjoka saw the bill from The Sultan's Resort in Anike's bag. The week before, she had gone for a retreat with her workmates in Aburi. Sai had dropped by and they had disappeared to the resort for some days. She should have thrown the bills and receipts away but she had forgotten all about them. They listed the exotic foods they had purchased, the spas they had been to…and everything was 'for two'. Adjoka raved and ranted about it, and she had fiercely defended herself.

"Where are you going?" he now demanded crossly. "Far away from you." she barked, and she stomped out.

She was shaking. She wanted to see Sai. He wouldn't nag or insult her like Adjoka did. Anike reached out for her handbag and brought out the small, sleek black box. Her heart warmed as she opened it. The rock on Sai's ring shone in the darkness. He had proposed to her that morning. Anike sighed in frustration. She would call her parents, tell them to return the traditional drinks to Adjoka's family and break up the marriage. She would run away at midnight. She would go to Sai and she would forget all about her uncouth husband.

She killed time by planning what to do. It was around eleven when she sneaked into their bedroom to get some clothes. She packed hastily. She was swift. She took her car keys and tiptoed to the garage. She sat in the car for a few minutes, her eyes closed. Adjoka meant she would stay home and work on her marriage. Sai meant she would leave. She chose Sai.

Anike drove like a woman possessed. She sped; she wove into dark, dangerous paths. She was livid. Adjoka had called her a whore and a liar. She had called him worse things. She was lost in thought. She heard some people shouting, but she only realized their shouts were directed at her when she saw the huge articulated truck coming towards her. She had not checked the traffic lights. She shrieked in fear, and tried to swerve to the next path but her brakes failed. Anike tried to get out of the car, but she felt like she had been glued onto her seat. She started screaming, and the articulated truck came for her. She saw the blinding white lights and sank into oblivion.

Anike felt someone pushing against her. There were whispers. There was heat. Gross discomfort. Wait. Why was she feeling anything? She was supposed to be dead. Her eyes popped open as she saw countless people flitting around. "Where am I?" she shrieked in alarm.

The raspy laugh made her jump. The man next to her whispered, "We're in the limbo of the Fathers. Purgatory. Afterlife. It's neither heaven nor hell, but very soon you'll know your stand and where you'll be sent to."

Painful tears welled up in her eyes. It was hell all the way. She never should have left home. It was her turn now. Anike felt a light tap on her shoulder. She refused to open her eyes. She knew it. She was going to hell. She was going to endure fiery torment for eternity. She deserved it. She couldn't stop crying.

"Anike, open your eyes." The voice was low and familiar. Adjoka. Adjoka was not in purgatory with her. So where was he speaking from?

Anike's eyes popped open in fright.

Adjoka was peering down at her. "Are you okay?"

Anike's eyes blurred. "Where am I? Where are we? Did you also die?" her voice was raspy. Adjoka shook his head. "We're in the garage. You fell asleep here. It's morning."

"No. I went out last night. The articulated..." her eyes were filled with tears. She felt numb. She was in the car. She was alive. Adjoka stood there for a moment, unsure of what to do. He finally opened the car door and picked her up. She closed her eyes as he took her to the bedroom. He tenderly undressed her and carried her to the bathroom. He filled the tub with water and slipped in some scented salts. She cried. She couldn't believe it. She was alive. She hugged Adjoka fiercely and he looked surprised, but pleased.

"I'm sorry for everything," she whispered.

"I'm sorry. I prayed for you throughout the night", he told her, kissing her forehead, his eyes wet with tears. As he turned to go, she whispered, "Adjoka. Come bath with me". He chuckled. "I thought you'd never ask."

Anike ended the affair with Sai. Something in the dream had changed her. It had been weeks since the devastatingly vivid dream. She and Adjoka were stuck in traffic. An articulated truck passed, and the driver winked at her. He looked like…like the guy who had been sitting next to her in purgatory. Anike's heart was beating. The traffic lights, her speeding, the accident. The death. Somehow, she knew it wasn't just a dream. Somehow, she knew she had been saved from purgatory.

For Girls Who Do Not Know What's Good for Them

Ama Asantewa Diaka

You're in the back seat of a rickety bright yellow bus. If you were a foreigner, you would have gripped the tattered seats like your life depended on it. But you've lived in this city all your life, you aren't going to die because this trotro sounds like it is ten minutes away from falling apart.

The bus pulls to a halt at your junction. All you want to do is crawl into bed and hide inside of yourself. But the neighbours talk, and the next thing you know, your mother is calling home asking why you're walking around town looking like she hasn't fed you since you hit puberty.

It's only when you're almost home that you realize how easy it is to smile at complete strangers. You inadvertently reach for the switch, but the lights are already on and your mother looks up at you with a smile.

It is Thursday. Why is she home on a Thursday?

You fake a smile and turn away, but she's too fast. One look at you and she can tell something is wrong.

"What's wrong?" she asks.

"Nothing, mother. How is your cough?"

You drop your bag in the worn out armchair and start peeling your clothes off.

She repeats the question. You're determined to brush this off too, but it's been a long day of pretending and suddenly, a nasty sounding sob erupts from your throat. It lasts for exactly fifteen seconds and you go back to peeling your clothes.

She pulls you to the bed and holds you for a full minute without saying a word. There's a short silence before she asks again what the problem is. You tell her it's nothing; you're just tired from work. She tells you she's not just your mother; she's your best friend. But you're too ashamed of your short-lived tears to utter a word, so you hold onto your claim of nothingness.

"Have you been jilted again?"

The word *jilted* tickles your insides, and, in spite of yourself, you start to laugh. Without saying another word, she knows.

She's holding you in her arms like you're twelve. She asks you to show her a picture of his face so she can poke out the loser's eyes through the phone.

Who dares break her daughter's heart?

You're trying to stifle a laugh but it's not working, your cheeks are too full of it. Soon you're both laughing.

She doesn't ask what happened or why.

She tells you about 1983, when there was no food in the country on account of the famine, and how everything became a luxury. Having sugar and milk was the same as having gold. People were using stones and old tuna tins to queue from Nyamekye all the way to Kaneshie for fermented corn dough.

There were such deep gorges around our collarbones that you could store buckets of water in them.

She tells you how on one fine Friday she stood in a queue to Mampong for four hours, only for the station master to allow another gentleman to take her seat. She complained bitterly and scowled the entire time, pained that she had to wait another two painful hours for the next car.

On reaching the spot after Aburi, in the neck of the hill was the very bus she'd missed, mangled up against a rocky hill, with onlookers rooted to the ground as bodies were being pulled from the damaged car.

How horrified and immediately forgiving she was.

Cudjoe was just like that bus you missed. You think you deserve it, you're sure it is meant for you, you toiled for it. Where did you go wrong? You stood in the damn sun for it. Of course, it is yours! But you missed it for a purpose. A better bus will come along. A better bus just for you.

You tell her, "But this was a better bus! This was a great bus! Why does it have to move without me? I want this bus!"

You want to tell her she would've loved Cudjoe. He was tender and handsome and true. He made you happy. He made you look forward to tomorrow. He made you dream.

But you don't. Because you don't have an answer
when she asks you why the bus left.

She shakes her head at you as if you're a toddler who doesn't know what's good for her. She kisses your hand and calls you her princess. You are boundless and infinitely tender. You're fierce and overwhelmingly gifted. She tells you not to let anybody's disregard for your essence impair your magnificence.

She says to you, "No daughter of mine misses a bus that's meant for her. One day, someone will come along who will want to die with you."

Who am I?

Amanda Olive Amoah

I wake up because the sun is shining on my face; I roll onto my side and peer at the alarm clock. Sigh. Its two hours till my alarm goes off. There's no point trying to go back to sleep so I jump out of bed and into the shower. Even though the rays have warmed me up, I turn up the hot water till I think I can smell my flesh cooking. And then I turn it off. I go to the sink to brush my teeth. There's a note on the mirror: "Walk the dog"

I have a dog?

As if on cue, I hear a loud bark. It sounds like a really big dog. I dress up in skinny jeans and a white t-shirt. I run my fingers through my damp hair and then stroll out of the bedroom. There is a pair of trainers outside the kitchen entrance. I pull them on over my bare feet and continue inside. The bark that greets me, reverberates throughout my body. I stumble and have to grab onto the kitchen island to keep from falling.

The dog bows his head (well, I think it's a he), and whines softly. He inches forward and licks my face. It is a feeling I remember. I laugh. I like it. I wrap my arms around his neck and bury my face in his fur. A tear runs down my cheek. He is such a big dog!

His head comes up to my chest when he sits down. He is huge! I can't tell what breed he is. He looks like he's many breeds put together; I see Alaskan malamute, German shepherd, and some Doberman. He's tethered to a chair and I untie him. The sound from his wagging tail sounds like a helicopter taking off. When I get to the door, I don't know what to do or where to go; nothing looks familiar. He walks forward and then sits down, politely turning to me. He is waiting.

I walk out and lock the door. He begins to walk forward slowly, ever so often turning around to make sure I'm following. I keep up, walking closely by his side. We walk down the street, and then around the block. The newspaper boy, the koko seller, the waakye seller and the seamstress all smile and wave at me. I don't remember their faces, but I manage a crooked uncertain smile anyway.

We come back to the house and I lock us in. We plop down in front of the telly and the news is on. After a while I'm waking up, I don't remember falling asleep. I walk to my bedroom and lay down in the bed. I'm tired. I fall asleep. My alarm wakes me. I roll to the other side of the bed and there's a note stuck to the pillow: "Feed the dog."

I have a dog?

I get out of bed and walk out of the room. Sure enough, there's a huge dog in front of the kitchen entrance, wagging a very big tail. He doesn't look dangerous. I walk forward cautiously anyway. He lets out a loud bark and stands up. I take a step back; he comes up to my waist. He licks my hands and nuzzles my palms. It is a feeling I remember. I like it. I smile. I wrap both my arms around his neck and bury my face in his fur. A tear runs down my cheek.

There's a huge dish on the kitchen island with the name Bartholomew printed in large bone designs. I smile and turn to him.

"Bartholomew" I say.

His ears perk up and he wags his tail with increased vigour. I look around and see a cabinet labelled: Bartholomew's Feast. I laugh, open it and take out a can labelled: Savoury beef and potatoes.

"Yum" I say to him.

I think he smiles up at me. There's a can opener next to his bowl. I set his food next to him and sit with my hand moving through his fur while he eats. I hear keys rattling, and then a key turns in the lock. I stiffen. Bartholomew licks my hand as if to calm me, and then goes back to his food. I stand up and walk to the kitchen entrance.

A tall, well-built, mocha-coloured young man enters. I grip the can opener tight in my hands and stand where I am. He's carrying a grocery bag. He looks at me; his eyes travel to the can opener in my hand. He smiles and takes a step forward.

"Hello mum, you alright?" his lips move, sounding out his words in an English accent. Mum?

Well he does look a lot like me… but I'm too young to have such a grown-up son; he must be at least thirty years old! And I'm only twenty-five.

"Are you from the future?" I ask. My hand shoots up to cover my mouth and my eyebrows are raised in surprise. Why?

Why do I speak with an English accent as well?

He walks up to me, hugs me with his free hand and gives me a kiss on the cheek. "No Mum, I'm not from the future," He walks past me into the kitchen.

I turn to face him, still gripping the can opener tightly in my hand. That's when I see it, my reflection in the glossy fridge. My midnight black dreadlocks have all gone grey. I've got wrinkles around my eyes and mouth.

Who am I?

Her Story

Amma Konadu Anarfi

They all said the story was going to end with the main character, Sharon, dead. They said she was going to break under a thick fog of depression and then overdose on some sleep meds. They also said long before the day she died, that she was going to suffer days and days of therapy, hospital stays…all the times when she'd stare at her tiny, pale wrists with a hunger so grave she had to marry her skin with steel blades, they had said it would happen.

They said she would not stay in school, what with all the voices in her head, she couldn't keep a thing of importance in there! She would get herself dismissed for assaulting school mates, teachers…even the janitor had his share.

Her parents were wealthy, they had a name—a standing in society. All eyes were on the family. Their daughter, Sharon, had to be hidden. They said they did…yes, they hid her in a facility not many people knew about. They said it was like Heaven tucked away in the heart of the country, bustling with frenzied activities; they said she was sent off without a tear from her mother, or a final glance from her father. They said Sharon was not even bothered, because she had never really known her parents… she had known the Nanny, the Butler and the Driver; *they* were her family, they said.

In that facility, there were only cold sheets and metal trays filled with colourful pills and syringes that rattled as they knocked against each other with each step the nurses took. They said she made no friends, made no eye-contact to see what lay in the eyes of the people she found there. She was scared of what she'd see, they said.

It was there she started painting again and they said it was a wonder to see her grace any canvas with her imagination. She breathed life into her paintings. It was like watching Mozart compose another masterpiece, they said, to see her at it, her hands and apron all stained with colour while she painted out the demons in her head and smiled at them when she was done.

They said she was so terribly fond of all her pieces that she'd sit for hours in her makeshift studio just watching them, a tiny smile playing around her lips, only to be broken by a twitch that caught the nurse's eye. She was going to lose it again, they'd say. Art couldn't keep her. They were right. She seemed to have gone colour-blind, for all of her paintings turned to shades before her mind and she would run into her studio to tear up her work, piece after piece, screaming out in a sound of terror that strum the strings of other people's hearts.

But they never talked about that silent observer in that facility, that one who one day could not take it anymore, who collected poor Sharon into his arms, rocking her back and forth.

They didn't say how she calmed and, for the first time in too many years looked into another person's eyes. They didn't say her tears stopped mid-way down her cheeks when she let her eyes melt into his, they didn't say. They *didn't*. A year and half of friendship they didn't say. Sharon fell in love with a man, but they did not say. The nurse had stolen her heart, but no one cared.

They failed, they *absolutely* failed to mention that he was running errands one rainy evening when the truck slid off the road and ran headlong into a parked trailer, killing him. They didn't say what pain shot through Sharon that very night for she knew as if by some divine vision that he was gone. They didn't say that was the day she rushed out into the studio, pulled out a fresh canvas and laid it flat on the floor, the very spot where they'd first made love, and spilled out all her tears, love, anger, hurt, frustration onto the canvas, a medley of wild, tangled emotions. They did not say.

When that piece of art ended up in a gallery two years later, along with much of her work, no one said that...no one said it. All they said, each time they stopped before that last piece of art that was her very soul poured out, was that they had known it would end that way.

Her parents took charge of all her pieces; they did, as well as all the money that they earned. Yet somewhere, in some foster home, where some of the money was channelled, lived a little girl who had her father's warm smile…and Sharon's eyes.

Tonight's Special

Amma Konadu Anarfi

You see, it is not as though he ever loved dogs. He had grown up having them for dinner instead. So, it really was surprising that he seemed taken so fondly to the jet black Havanese that nibbled at one of the handles of the skipping rope she often liked to use. *She* was Foriwaa, with full hips and a backside pushed into yoga pants; those brown pants that made her look naked, and the halter top that gently rested over her rather tiny breasts.

The skipping rope was right where she had left it the last time she used it—half-hidden under the double settee and half-cushioned by the rag on which the fluffy little dog lay, engrossed in his nibbling.

What happened was quite sad. Sampson would have married her, had she not packed and left him right after sweating all over the living room floor, after skipping in every corner of that space that morning. It was the day after Valentine's, three days after their 9th anniversary, and about 18 hours after he had brought the dog home as a gift for her.

He knew exactly where she packed off to. Foriwaa! Nine years of dating and a preceding three of friendship in his undergrad years had taught him too much about her, too much that left no room for surprises. Complex was Foriwaa—independent and dependent. Why, she got offended whenever Sampson even remotely hinted at marriage. Nonconformist, she called herself! Why the hell was she running off to tie the knot with someone she was not supposed to like? The very person about whom she had ranted for hours after she returned home from a corporate dinner a year ago!

"Such a dog! Thinking he could just have his way with me. I could file a report for sexual harassment! Why, he didn't just open the door for me, he placed his hand on the small of my back and the smirk … that smirk! Gosh, I just knew what he was thinking!"

This very man Foriwaa swore to hate forever, she had packed, and was running off to! The dog yapped on for a while and began a tussle with the curtain, as the fabric moved with the air that swept into the room. Sampson sat and stared, unblinking.

He would admit any day, that the dog was a desperate move to make Foriwaa stay. You see, five years into their relationship she had decided to tie her tubes. It was her body, to do with as she pleased. No man would have her popping babies out of her vagina.

The dog had now tired and lay down panting happily, staring back at Sampson, who for the last hour had barely blinked.

One year had Foriwaa getting 'softer', Sampson would say; she started wearing brighter colours. The first time he saw her in a floral summer dress, he nearly passed out. He had been so used to seeing her in browns and greys and too many blacks. He had ceased to imagine that there were other colours she could actually dress up in. He couldn't wrap his head around the change. Foriwaa was suddenly 'girlier' than she had ever been and uncomfortably secretive. She had never been one to hide anything!

9 years! God! Who wouldn't have followed her all the way to the untarred, deserted road that led to the highway? Who wouldn't have flagged her down, knowing she would stop? There was no way he was going to let her move in with someone who was everything he was not. It had been his pleasure to carry her back inside. It could have been their wedding night.

She shouldn't have left like that. After all the work he had put into loving her. Leaving him for the same man she had called chauvinist so many times. Not that he had changed, or that Sampson had changed, but *she* had!

So, he bought the dog; for her. Why? She had forever wanted a fluffy little black dog she could name Dracula. Dracula! Sampson's eyes watered as he stood, gaze still fixed on the happy dog, moving towards it, determinedly.

Foriwaa's laughter rang in his head. How the name had fascinated her! Dracula.

When the police got there, he was seated at table, the house dead silent, having dinner; spiced ribs and red wine. Dracula. Sampson smiled, dropped the cutlery, wiped his lips and presented his hands to be handcuffed. He was calm, waiting as they searched. He knew they only needed to open his refrigerator to find what they were looking for: Foriwaa and three quarters of the dog he never loved – grilled.

Africa Calling Card

Anakwa Dwamena

For now, you relish scratching the silver back of the four calling cards you just paid for, with a nickel out of your $1.37 in change. One card is to call home, twenty minutes should be enough—if the conversation goes over, that's fine. Your call after, to the pastor, shouldn't last long anyway. The other two are for old schoolmates. The boys; Boakye if he will be home, and Junior who is always home, and then Eunice, and then Maame Yaa, who you know will talk the longest.

You can't ever imagine losing the exhilaration of being on the other side! You are suddenly aware of the battered and bulky bags that line the side of your room, the stretches and streaks in the carpet from the dragging of luggage and work boots, both feet dangling above the lower bunk bed where your roommate would be, were he not at his night shift. If you are feeling inspired, you will plop down and pace over to the window, looking out at America, or the backyards of America at least.

You can't ever imagine forgetting the noise surrounding the call, when you yourself had once been on that other side. There is the ball bouncing against the walls, outside, in the daily battle for football bragging rights; the collective inhalation and exhalation of the streets. If it is afternoon (Ghana time) the proud call and response of pestles in neighbouring houses (the Ntow's eat fufu every evening), the neighbour's baby not whispering her displeasure at one thing or another, and the banging of the door as one of your little siblings rushes to answer the ringing phone.

Even without trying, you can still hear the sounds from the bedroom best, the excitedly repeated "hello, hello" and borderline shouting. It is in this room you waited your turn to talk to your brother, debating whether to ask for shoes or a video game. Whether to let him know now, or wait till he was settled. Maybe he hadn't saved enough money yet. But then again, it was America, there could surely be no shortage of money.

You can't ever imagine the name America no longer exciting you, even now that you are here. Friends used to laugh at you when you said you were going soon, and haters mocked you by calling you "Borga". But since you left, your Facebook inbox does not winnow their messages. All the messages make you feel special.

In the old days, on your walk back to the house, between the barber and the barman, at the pharmacy store and among the area boys, you would answer that your brother is doing fine, with a nod and a shy smile, knowing the respect his migration has already leveraged for you.

You can't ever imagine that you will not call home for months. That your little sister, will no more relish waiting her turn in line to speak with you, in hope that your credits do not run out. That she will not notice how heavy the telephone feels and how arcane it looks compared to the smartphones today. She will not ask herself whether she really has been a "good girl" since your last call, or regret her last lie about being one.

Even without trying, you can answer when people ask about the last time you talked to the family; "three days ago", with a confident smile, since it sounds better than 3 months.

You wonder how you became so busy, how the only times you are off work are too early or too late to call home. How can you explain why you haven't called in a long time, and why you haven't sent anything you promised?

When you come across a calling card under your bed while cleaning one day, you will try to imagine what home must be like now. Are the children still playing football outside or are they pounding fufu now? You hope everyone is doing well, by God's grace, just as you are.

The Weight of the World

Ato Kwamena Bentsil

It's been three days. I have had the same terrifying dream. Each night after the first, the dream starts over but lasts longer, with more details than the previous night's.

Father says the gods are trying to tell me something. His father, who was high priest before him, saw the gods when he was my age, and he also, had his calling when he was only a boy. It has become my responsibility, then, to stay asleep through the nightmare and yield my soul without fear to the ancestors and gods so they can fully reveal what they have been trying to tell these past few days. Father said as high priest he could sense it, and that it was urgent, a matter of life and death—that I might just save a life or serve a bigger purpose such as saving the entire village.

Mother says she knew a day like that would come, right after she pushed me out of her womb, when Maame Akyaah laid me in her arms and she saw the hump on my back. She knew then that the whole world lay on my back and I would have to bear its weight always and carry it to safety someday.

She says it is the reason why the villagers treat me so specially, the reason why they give me my own space wherever I go so I can enjoy the fresh air. And it is the same reason why the market women refuse to sell to me. They believe the shoulders that carry the weight of the world should not be laboured with such trivialities as cassava tubers and tomato fruits. Their husbands and children avoid me for fear of the hump on my back but mother says its reverence for my destiny.

Three days ago, I was loitering around the edge of the evil forest, near the house of Father Moses, the Catholic priest. He saw me and invited me to talk for the first time ever. He treated me in a special way - more pleasant than the villagers ever did. He laughed at my name 'Paa Baadu' and said he would call me 'Abraham' instead. Father Moses went on to read to me the story of Abraham and his descendants from a book he called Bible. When I told Mother of my new friend, she banned me from his company, saying he did not revere my destiny, for the priest had said it was not the weight of the world I carried; that I was only a hunchback. "His god is also strange; different from the gods to which your father is a high priest", and she would hear no more of Father Moses.

The weight of the world feels heavier tonight than any other night of my life. Even though father says I must yield to the gods, I am afraid to close my eyes and sleep. I am afraid the dream will return and terrify me. But the night is quiet and the stars mutedly watch on from above. Even the crickets aren't haggling in their night business and I drift unwillingly to sleep with the breeze of the darkness.

Father Moses is with me again, this time with two other men in white robes. There is chaos in the village. A man has just been killed. He lies motionless in the village centre with blood oozing from his nose and eyes. They say he was struck down by the gods. I run over and realize it is my father. My heart pounds hard against my chest and I run screaming towards our hut. The shrill of someone's laughter terrifies me. It is Father Moses, "He was a fool my dear Abraham, all who do not believe in my God are fools and eternal punishment awaits them".

I wanted to wake up but my consciousness was trapped in my dream. The gods have…no…God has spoken his message but refuses to free my yielded soul. Hands clutch me and shake me violently. "Paa Baadu! … Paa Baadu!" I wake up to father's grasp and Mother's ghostly stare. "What did you see? …What did you see Paa Baadu?" "I … I … I saw the weight of the world," I reply ominously.

Homework

Daniel Hanson Dzah

Assembly.

Arms forward stretch. Arms sideways stretch. One *logologo* line.

Inspection. Neat collar. Clean handkerchief. Let me smell your armpit. White singlet. White socks. Black shoe. Brown shoe. White socks. Black camboo. Brown camboo. White socks. Black sandals. Brown sandals. Where is your badge? *Whip-whip-whip!*

"God bless our Homeland Ghana." "I promise on my honour." "Our Father who art in Heaven." "And can it be." "Fairest Lord Jesus." "We are marching to our classes."

'Good Morning Class.' 'Good Morning Sir.' 'How are you?' 'We are fine, thank you. And yoouuu?' 'Sit down. Where is your homework?'

'It was too difficult, sir.' 'Father left my book in his car boot, sir.' 'Father did not sign, sir.' Teacher *banza*. Driver *banza*. Father *banza*. *Whip-whip-whip!*
Morning drill.

Students' Companion. Companion of teachers. Foe of students. Homonyms. Bear. Bear. Bank. Bank. Homophones.

Key. Quay. See. Sea. Antonyms. Arrive-Depart. Adore-Despise. Attack-Retreat.

Synonyms. Abandon-Leave-Desert. Astonished-Surprised-Perplexed. Flabbergasted? *Whip- whip-whip!*

Collections. A bunch of? Bananas! A troupe of? Monkeys! A bouquet of? Err…err. *Whip- whip-whip!* You monkey!

Mental. Square root of? LCM of? HCF of? 12 Squared plus 5 Squared minus 15 Squared plus 10 Squared minus 2 Squared times zero? *Whip-whip-whip!*

Break time please!

Auntie please one bread. One meat-pie. One rock buns. One *bofroat*. Tampico. Fan Yoghurt. Fan Chocolate. Fan Pop. Fanice…so nice, nice, nice.

Green green grasses. Kwaku Ananse Stories. Change your style. Change your style. Be like that. Be like that. Boys play football. Girls play Ampe. *Mother jeega nobody!*

Break over please!

School Prefect. Compound Prefect. Bell boy. Cupboard Monitor. Blackboard Cleaner. Class Prefect: Sweeping Roster. Class Prefect: Names of talkatives. Kojo Mensah -DP. Adwoa Mansa - TP. Your head is hard. Your head is hard *paa*!

Midterm.

Midterm Break. Midterm Holidays. Midterm Homework. English Homework. Mathematics Homework. Social Studies Homework. Integrated Science Homework. Agricultural Science Homework. Technical Drawing Homework. Catering Homework. Graphic Design Homework. French Homework. Ga Homework. Twi Homework. No-break Midterm. No-holiday Midterm.

You like that *paa*. You too you like that *paa*! You are someway *papa*. You too you are someway *papa*! I won't say anything. Me I won't talk. I'm going to come. I'm coming. I'm coming right now, okay? Go tear, it is sweet. *Herh!* Who spoke vernacular? Only English! Speak only English!

Who Fla-tu-lat-ed? Flatulence. Farts. Boys at the back. Maybe girls at the front. Do females fart? Does Queen Elizabeth fart? Who knows? We never know. Nobody ever knows.

Farts. Silent farts. Loud farts. Smelly farts. Korle Lagoon farts. Lavender Hill farts. Oblogo borla farts.

Mosquito romance. Tease the girls. Chase the boys. Chase him all around the classroom. Slap him in the back! Pinch his arm! Oh, no! There is a teacher! Oh, yes! *There's* a teacher! Sir, he was teasing me. He was teasing me, Sir. I don't like that. I do not like that-o. *Yoo.*

Our day. Digestive. Hob Nobs. Rich Tea. Shortbread. Coke. Fanta. Sprite. Oh, gimme some of your Malt ehh?

Speakers. Microphone. DJ. Dancing Floor. Dancing Competition. Jams. Who let the dogs out? Wo! Wo! Wo-wo-wo! Oh nananaana! It is our day!

Vacation classes. Vacation Classwork. Vacation Homework. Home-work. Go home and work.

The Message

Daniel Hanson Dzah

They slowly make their entrance. The adults stroll in, flanked by their children. They heartily hug me and shake my hand—the adults. I recognise their faces. I smile at them. Then they present the children, reminding me of the particulars: names, ages, where they were outdoored. The children make an effort to hug me. I make a point to ask their names again. As before, I instantly forget the answers.

I beam at these grandchildren, my grandchildren. But I remain focused on a more pertinent realisation: Every tiny part of their little faces reminds me of my long-dead siblings.

There are more bodies entering the living room as more leave. I notice this as I hug another grandchild. "Tutuwa," her mother announces before I ask, and I soon remember I need to go to the bathroom. I call out for Maafia. She rushes to my side and immediately understands. She explains to the rest of the families and guides me to the bathroom, my arm locked in hers.

I return to unusually loud laughter in the living room. I squint and discover that Ebo is here. He realises my entry and explodes in an unwelcome remark. Something about me and "sweet sixteen". He adds irreverently that he would most definitely hit on me unawares if he saw me randomly somewhere in the streets. I smile in embarrassment. It must be the transparent upper part of my kaba. There is also my failure to prevent Maafia from plastering her entire tub of foundation make-up on my face. Typical Ebo, always drawing unsolicited attention to whomever he desires. I politely ignore him to find my seat.

More reintroductions, more pressure on my limited memory. I cling unto the faces of the children for hope. Somewhere in them, I can see my siblings. My eldest sister Ohenewaa here, the second-born Kyerewaa over there, even the ever-shy Asiedua over there. My only brother Atiemo shows up in a 4-foot body and almost upends me with his hug. I laugh heartily and ask his name. I ask for his mother. He leans back to point at my fourth daughter. I smile in acknowledgment—she was always my favourite.

Little Atiemo hugs me again and draws my shoulders down to his height. In the midst of the expressions of adoration by the adults in the room, he whispers softly into my right ear. I am not sure I hear him right, so I make an effort to pull out of the hug to stare him in the face. The little boy does not loosen his grip. He whispers again and a calm warmth slowly creeps over me and causes me to smile. Now I am sure of it. My siblings are here today.

The Happy Birthdays were sang, exclaimed, chirped, belched, danced, clapped, sobbed, pecked and hugged out to me. They said their goodbyes and left their presents with Maafia. The house is empty now. The families are all gone. It was nice to see all of them so happy, even Ebo. I am proud of myself. I have given them my best. Ninety years have been enough. My siblings came here to remind me of that.

I smile as Maafia helps me onto my bed and gently rests my head on the pillow. "Medaase Maafia. Nyame nhyira wo bebree," I say softly to her, while squeezing her hand firmly with mine. She walks out and I smile to myself, as I am again surrounded by faces, faces ready to take me with them. Faces from long ago. Familiar faces. Smiling faces. I close my eyes.

A Beer for Frederick

Edem Dotse

"For me, if I have life? Health? That's real riches to me."

Frederick's words would hang over my lumpy hospital bed as I lay silently, with nothing to do but stare at the slow drip of dextrose in the IV bag, with the stench of penicillin on my breath.

The topic had come up one lazy afternoon, in between gulps of Star beer. The sun spilled through the gaps in the roof of Maame Serwaa's Spot, and wiry chickens pecked away at the gravel at our feet. I would always have a harmless coke, not because I wanted a clear head for the next lecture, but because Frederick ordered it for me the first time he found the place, and I wanted to indulge him. I had always wanted to indulge him.

The topics were always random. Occasionally, a stranger would chime in to his rants about women, prices in Accra, or whatever occupied his mind at the time. I would mumble a few words in agreement, but having been dragged out of the hostel, my mind was always stuck in whatever textbook I had left behind.

"Hey!" he would shout, waving a meaty hand at me each time I zoned out, "Where your mind dey?"

I was the diligent, promising student and he was the carefree, womanizing miscreant whose aspirations stretched outside of the degree we were pursuing. Somehow, we meshed. His constant chatter drowned out the thoughts in my own head. Every vacation I would promise him a visit in Wa, upon his offering. Of course, I knew I would never make the trip.

Komla, my ward mate in the hospital, was a successful water engineer from Dabala, who spoke fluent Russian and got his bachelor's degree two years before I was born. We would talk of his projects across the Volta, why the government did not budget enough money for good water regulation, his son's love for basketball (and hatred for education), as well as how to get into large-scale farming.

"I've never been on admission my whole life—fifty-five good years." Komla said after a long period of silence.

"Sickness makes one realize what's really important in life."

Frederick would later inform me—in between mouthfuls of Tuo Zaafi—that he would not be returning to school the following week, or to Accra. That the borehole beneath his father's compound would soon become a lucrative pure water business for him. I had hung up the phone with a wry smile.

Instead of class, that day, I stopped by Maame Serwaa's place and ordered two beers. One for me, and one for Frederick.

Airtel Five

Edem Dotse

Glasses and Credit—those were the first two things that came into Mawuli's mind when he woke up. He smelled like red earth and felt like he hadn't taken a shower in days. He lifted his dirt-crusted face and peered around.

It was a full minute before he realized he was lying by the side of a major road. The rushing sound of a huge truck had startled him into alertness, causing him to sit up. The blazing glare of the sun forced him to shield his face with his right hand. He had no idea where he was. He could not recollect the previous day's events. The noise of cars whizzing by him confused him even more.

Where was he? Not too far from where he worked, he believed. Yes, he must have been going home, or somewhere in the area. Either that or he was completely lost- he couldn't be certain. His eyes scanned past the sea of vehicles, looking for familiar landmarks.

Something had happened the previous night. He was sure—or at least he thought he was sure. He knew it involved glasses and credit, but for the life of him, could not recall exactly what. He tried to form a picture in his mind from fragmented thoughts.

Glasses. He felt inside his coat pocket, but his fingers pinched an empty groove in the silky fabric where the horn-rimmed spectacles should have been. This prompted him to rise to his feet, searching all his pockets. He found a cell phone in another compartment of the coat.

He looked up at the sun, almost in the centre of the sky. It was noon. He was hours late for work, and would have to call in and explain. But explain what? He didn't understand himself.

He hadn't noticed the construction workers digging around him until just then. Most were minding their business, but some were looking in his direction, and laughing. Instinctively, he moved towards them. They began watching him closely, smiles hidden on their faces. One of them finally said, "Maa Adwoa is not here oh," and chuckled.

Maa Adwoa. The name registered something in his mind. "Maa Adwoa?" He looked at the fellow. "Where is Maa Adwoa?" He was not sure why he was looking for her. His question went unanswered. He took slow, uneasy steps across the steaming red sand, unable to see properly without his glasses. Did Maa Adwoa have them? Is that what had happened?

No, he resolved. The last place he would have left his glasses was the office, and his secretary would have picked them up.

He tried to check the phone for her number but it wasn't there. His account balance was empty and he could not call anyone.

Credit. It suddenly dawned on him. Maa Adwoa was the credit seller, not too far from his office. He must have been going there to recharge. His pace quickened. He had to get to her, and he knew she was close by.

The sight of the familiar blue hue of her umbrella, albeit unfocused in his eyes, made his heart warm. He began calling out to her, "Maa Adwoa! Maa Adwoa!" He had drawn the attention of everyone around him, but he did not care. He was too relieved. He would talk to Maa Adwoa, call the office and explain everything. Everything would be fine.

Serwaa saw the madman coming again and sighed. It wasn't that she was not used to it—he came everyday—but it made her morning a little more depressing every time. He was nothing but a slight nuisance on most days. Indeed, Maa Adwoa had insisted that he wouldn't be any trouble when she took over the stand from her two years ago. Poor Maa Adwoa—she still blamed herself partly for the accident that day that left his mind disoriented, stuck in a loop. Maybe that was why she left.

She dealt with him every day—he was like a regular customer. He would appear in his mud brown suit covered in dirt—a suit he hadn't taken off for the past three years—asking for *credit* with a story about his secretary. Then he would attempt to load it into his phone, which of course didn't work. He would give up eventually, and then wander the streets looking for his office which had closed down years ago. He would eventually give that up too—or be escorted away by security at the building—and leave. She didn't know where he went, but he always came back. She tried several times to explain it all to him, but he didn't get it. Maa Adwoa tried too. But of course, they had both given up.

"Maa Adwoa," he called out. She hadn't noticed he was already by her side. "Mawuli," she smiled—the type of smile that hides faint sadness.

"Me pa wo kyew, ma me—"

"Airtel," she cut him off, as she did nowadays. "Yes, air—" "—airtel five cedis," she handed him a used recharge card. He would not know the difference.

He tried to explain when he couldn't find any money, but she waved him away. She let him stand under the cool shade of the umbrella, fumbling with his card and his phone. Then she watched him walk away finally, shaking her head sadly.

Kenkey for Ewes

Edem Dotse

Evenings with Nkansah would always culminate like this; horseplay fuelled by alcohol, and us sitting in his car parked outside my house. He would talk excitedly about how beautiful the country was becoming, how he felt more and more like a stranger each time he returned. I would laugh and remind him that the rubbish heaps behind McCarthy Hill were still as high as ever. He would smirk and pinch me chidingly.

I sat idly peeling at the corners of a sticker on a mug—a tacky gift from the wedding we attended hours earlier. Managing a large rip across the face of the bride and groom, I squealed with joy as he snatched it away from me.

"Why would you do that?" he asked, feigning anger. "What?"
"It looks better now."
"Don't be a hater, Sefakor."

"Ah? Why would I hate on that sham of a marriage? Everyone knows he's been sleeping around since they started dating."

The mug went limp in his hands. "Seriously?"
"*Eeeeverybody* knows. I give them five years. Less than five years koraa, you watch." Nkansah remained silent.

"So negative. This is why my mother doesn't like you," he said finally, smiling coyly.

"Nonsense—my mother hates you too!" I giggled, pinching him back at last.

I changed the subject back to Accra. His gestures became animated again, exaggerated in the moonlight as he explained his ideas. These were exciting times, he said. There was so much industrial potential—acres of arable land that stretched from the motorway to the borders. He would bring investors next time. He was already drawing up contracts and making phone calls to his father's friends.

I smiled faintly.

"You're not the same anymore, you know," he stared intensely at me. "What? "I'm a beautiful young woman now?" I quipped. "Mtchew. Seriously, I don't know… just different."

"Look, I'm proud of you, Nkansah. I've always been. And I have your back… but…"
"But what?"
"…never mind."

More silence. I began to feel guilty.

"Your food is in the back seat oh—don't forget."

I already knew he wouldn't. Nkansah's love for Fante kenkey
was both amusing and endearing. His curious enthusiasm for
the world he had missed out on—having grown up in New
Jersey—rang to me as experimental. It seemed tourist-like, for
the sake of storing memories one would soon leave behind. Of
course, it was neither a fair assessment nor the product of a
rational train of thought. But, nowadays, I didn't know what to
think.

I stepped out of the car and leaned in through the open
window, exchanging one last long glance with Nkansah. He
stretched out his arm and pulled my cheeks playfully, trying to
distract me from the fact that he was unnerved. A little
disappointed too maybe, I noted.

"I have to make some akple for you when you come back…" I
said, stroking his shoulder gently.

"Some what?"
"Akple."
"What the hell's that?"

I sighed, suppressing my smile. "It's like kenkey for Ewes…"

Warfare

Edem Dotse

My mistake was not waiting for instructions from the other side. Without clearance, I shot up into the night sky, my thick black hair flapping against my face. Times had changed, and we did not usually fly out at night on Thursdays or Fridays. It was too dangerous. I had heard too many tales about deadly encounters with warring angels to be so foolhardy. But I was desperate. I knew I was running out of time and I had to complete my assignment. My host was becoming unsettled. I could feel her, restless in her sleep as the grisly details of the night unfurled in her mind as a dream.

It was a bleak rainy evening. I was on my way back from a meeting in Dzodze with the group of elder witches who hired me concerning a stubborn relative—known simply as 'the target'—who was impeding the progress of my assignment in the life of my host. Several suggestions were thrown around, including sickness and financial setback. However, we could not decide on anything conclusive.

I felt my body jerk violently amidst the clouds. I delved into my mind, feeling for the connection with my host. She was decidedly disturbed. But her moans and grunts were distant. I dipped lower into the atmosphere to navigate from the clouds. I thought it might be the turbulence distracting me. But our link seemed to be growing thinner with each passing moment. I did not understand why.

Then, I felt it. It was faint but clear, like heat radiating from a light bulb in a ceiling. There was another being in the sky.

I was not prepared for a fight. I flew higher up into the clouds, hoping they would cloak me. Whatever it was, it was getting closer. I could feel it getting closer.

The connection to my host dropped before I knew what was happening. Something was wrong. She had woken up. I began to panic. The link would come back in short flashes every now and then from her thoughts, but I could not piece together what was happening. So, as dangerous as it was, I shut my eyes and let the night dissolve around me, until all I saw and felt from the external world was nothing.

Darkness… Flash! Walking, Stairs… Streets… Cars, traffic…

The series of images came in quick flickers, akin to the death of a fluorescent light, declining in pace and intensity. Bits of disjointed sound came in the same way. I focused as hard as I could, but she was awake, and miles away. I would get nothing. Amidst the chaos, I heard a voice I recognized. A voice that filled me with dread. It was the target.

And that was when I felt the push.

I was sent spiralling downwards in the sky by a shove from a huge creature. I looked above me as I fell to see a silhouette of wings in the distance. I spun around as quickly as I could and flew back up. There was nowhere to go in the open sky. I had to fend off the angel or I wouldn't stand a chance.

Rising up in the sky, I saw a blur rushing towards me. This was no ordinary angel, he had incredible speed. I summoned all the force within me and fired a blast of energy through my right hand. He swiftly dodged, delivering a punch to my face. I was sent reeling backwards. In my confusion, I could still hear fragmented voices.

Break! Break every chain!

The angel was rushing up towards me. I spun out of his way and fired a blast of energy into his back. The resulting explosion sent him hurtling higher up into the skies. I spread out my arms for balance and stretched them towards him, waiting till he descended into my crosshairs. I began powering up energy through my arms. I would finish him off, here and now.

"Arghh!" I felt a searing surge in my right shoulder, which knocked me off balance. As my arms flailed in free fall, I felt more pain shoot through my right thigh and screamed out. I looked down to see the tip of a steel broadhead, glowing red hot, sticking out of my bloodied leg.

There was another angel.

We send arrows! Arrows to scatter the enemy!

The arrows came in quick succession of each other. I twisted my frame so that I would begin to fall headfirst and get a closer look. My injured shoulder made it difficult to navigate. I felt weaker and weaker as I fell.

We arrest every opposing force!

The angel had descended upon me, gripping me tightly. I was beginning to lose consciousness. I felt my body being pulled, and its wings flapping above me. Suddenly, there was a sharp pain in my head. The connection to my host was back, and stronger than it had ever been. I finally realized what was happening. I would not make it.

It was all over.

Evil spirit, we command you—leave her! Leave her!

"They marked her for death. But they will not get her. I say they will not get her!" the pastor cried out.

Ewurabena's eyes opened. She gasped and began panting heavily, realizing where she was— lying on the floor at the All-Night deliverance service. Yao, who had invited her, was standing in the distance, praying loudly. She sat up, with tears in her eyes, enchanted by the sounds of the organ. She was still breathing heavily, from the horrible, horrible nightmare she'd had.

The pastor took her by the hand and lifted her up into a teary embrace as the audience applauded.

"It's alright," he said, "It's alright. You are free."

The Things That Came with The Light

Ewurama Amoonua Adenu-Mensah

I lift a handful of sea water to my face and cringe as it settles into the rubbed-raw cracks underneath my eyes. But I do not feel the sharp stinging I prepared for. I do not feel anything. I look up and squint and hope that what I had just seen was merely a sleep-induced hallucination. But it is still there, and it still shines, a light brighter than anything I have ever seen.

I must be dying.

I scoop up more handfuls of the cool water and this time I wash my entire face. The water shoots painfully up my nostrils and I feel a coppery saltiness course down my tongue. I sink down onto the shallow sea bed and the wet sand shifts to accommodate my bony form. I briefly contemplate praying to the *ɛpo sunsum* but I get an immediate sense that even the sea god cannot command this one away. It feels far too real, far too close. It's certainly much too late for a prayer.

"Ato, bɛsen ma yɛnkɔ", I hear my friend Atta call from beyond the grove of palm trees we lay under to watch the sea at night. I hear heavy panting and the retreating slaps of bare feet against soaked earth as he continues to call for me to join him run back into the village to tell someone, anyone of this light charging steadily in my direction.

I feel it come closer and yet I do not move. I cannot move. It is mesmerizing, this growing brightness. I truly must be dying.

I am humbled by this light. It is brighter than a thousand fishermen lamps held together, faster than Paa Quansah's paddles during the Bakatue canoe races, scarier than the fetish priests performing the morning rituals. I do not move. I cannot move. I simply stare at it.

I am definitely dying.

I decide to resign to my fate. The gods must want me back and I am not about to challenge their authority. I feel the cool water seep into every inch of my cloth as I lower myself with my arms spread out and lift my knees off the soft sand of the shallow sea bed until I am floating. I close my eyes bravely, awaiting the next phase of the dying process.

I feel a sharp jerk and the tender flesh under my arms and above my rib-cage throbs. I know that when you die, your soul has to leave your body but I never thought this would be an actual physical process. Interesting. I wonder which other part of dying will turn out to be much different than I imagined.

I hear the garbled commands of a voice that sounds remotely like my father's but I am not entirely sure. This out-of-body experience is amazing. Maybe I am at my funeral, and maybe the voice is the last call to my dead body to rise before I am mistakenly buried alive. I hear it happens sometimes. I wish that this call would work, that I can wake up and run into my mother's arms. She is probably weeping bitterly, my poor mother. I am her only son. But I cannot change the ways of Death and as much as I want to stay, I must leave. It's funny how I don't even know where I am headed but I know it's only a matter of time.

I feel a heavy pressure on my back and it builds steadily with every passing second. Maybe it's the mud piling up on my back. I am surely being buried. The pressure builds. It feels surprisingly very real, almost painful even. It's crazy how real this all feels, these processes of dying. I always thought death would be painless. The pressure still builds. This is more painful than I thought it would get, this steady thudding at my back.

"Ato, bue w'enyiwa".

Definitely my father's voice, a little too coherent, a little too close. He wants me to open my eyes. The heavy threat looming in those three words he speaks is enough to scare me into trying. My eyes open just as his fist crashes into my lower back and I let out a strange, strangled sound. I am not dead.

I follow his eyes to see the light that shocked me into thinking the gods were calling me. It's attached to a Big Canoe, a looming wooden structure wedged in the wet sand at the shore.

In the dark, I make out the figures of other men from our village craning their necks from their crouched positions behind the thick-stemmed palms to watch the Big Canoe.

A thing emerges from behind the light and I hear the quickly gathering breaths of confused people. It looks like a man, two hands and two long legs like my father's. But it is different. Its skin looks like the inside of a freshly cut yam and its hair runs down its back in waves, just like the sea. It reaches the shore and we stare in puzzled amazement. And then it screams.

After it screams, other things like it jump down from the Big Canoe and tread towards the shore. The last thing I notice is the different colours of their hairs as my father yanks me up from his lap and drags me along, barely missing the palm trees. On his face is a look of pure panic, possibly terror. I have never seen him look so scared. We speed as fast as our legs can carry us to the house of the king to tell him about the things we just witnessed on the shore. The king must know what they are. He knows everything.

Keeping Up Appearances

Fui Can-Tamakloe

Whenever our 'busy' schedules would allow, we'd meet up at Eddie's Bar to catch up on the latest feats we had achieved in our separate kingdoms. We were still *The Three Crabs* to whoever remembered us from our days of jumping our school fence to buy some palm wine underneath the Neem tree next to Red's Car Workshop. Red was no longer there, and neither was the tree. But from the way you'd hear us go on about the fun we had during those days, you'd walk out of Eddie's Bar expecting to find the old Neem tree sitting tall and proud in the corner. You'd expect to see Sweetie underneath the tree, jealously guarding her pot of gold, and dishing out some of the good stuff.

We relived our memories during the nights at Eddie's Bar. We'd laugh at Collins' predicament when he thought he had impregnated Pastor Ntim's daughter, and Nartey's stammering that became very serious any time we were in trouble—which was always. We'd try to count the number of times we had been dragged to school half-drunk by some concerned parent. We'd laugh with some regret at how frequently our mothers had to make trips to the school to beg for us not to get expelled. "*If they are in school, they spend only half the day drinking. If you sack them from school, they'll spend the whole day drinking. Is that better?*" Nartey would mimic his own mother's words for our merriment. That's how we had earned the name The Three Crabs. Because crabs, very much like drunk people, could never walk in a straight line.

When we were done dredging up old memories, we'd talk about the present. Nartey would tell us about some new business he was working on that would fetch him millions in revenue. Collins would regale us with stories about how much he hated his job at the bank and how he was only still working there because of this one chick he hadn't yet shagged. I'd in turn tell them of the cocoa farm that I had inherited from an uncle and how the price for the product was increasing year after year.

Nartey lived off his aunt somewhere in Accra. Collins worked in a post office and not in a bank, and he couldn't quit his job even if he wanted to. Me? I'd messed up my chances of owning a cocoa farm a long time ago.

And when the guys had had their fill of beers and khebab one of us always miraculously paid for, they'd leave me behind in the bar. I'd quietly slink into the back, slip on an apron and continue washing the glasses and plates of people who were keeping up appearances too, one way or the other.

Marie

Fui Can-Tamakloe

She came to the hospital a broken-spirited girl; the tumour in her brain neared its expiry date. She spoke to no one, not even the doctors who tried to help her. Everyone said she had given up. But not me. I was the first one she spoke to, they say. Strange though, that the first person she'd spoken to was a hospital janitor well past his retirement age, who worked in the Intensive Care Unit. I remember the night clearly.

I was mopping the floor of her room when I heard her shift in bed. The poor thing; she was the most beautiful helpless girl I had ever seen. She was watching me mop the floor. Her eyes, they still haunt me now. In them was desolation. But that desolation seemed to be countered by the vestiges of cheerfulness and energy. She had been a very happy girl before all of this, it seemed. I grunted in her direction, as a way of apologizing for waking her up. Dragging the mop trolley, I attempted to make my exit. I didn't want to be in the same room with a dying person, seeing as I was quite advanced in years.

"Do you know what it's like to be dying?"

The question was asked so innocently. It wrenched my heart to realize that it came from such a young girl.

"I've known that feeling since I turned 65," I reply, in a gruff voice. I can't handle being in the room. I've worked long enough at the hospital to know not to talk to dying patients. It made their deaths routine and impersonal. I try to leave again. My fingers are on the door handle when she speaks again.

"I'm dying," she states simply. My grip on the door handle slackens a bit. "We all are," I say, "from the time we were born." I mean only to be frank.

"Do you mind sitting with me? I can't sleep," she says. *Silly girl. Who invites a complete stranger to sit by them?* This was the final room to mop, so I find myself shuffling over to the vacant chair by her bed.

"Thank you," she whispers. I shrug. Then we lapse into a minute of silence, but for the beeping of the life support machine.

"So… aren't you going to tell me your name?" I ask her, simply to make conversation. She relaxes on the pillow propped up behind her. She looks at me shyly.

"Tell me yours first."

"Fair enough. I'm Thomas, but you can call me Oluu. Everyone calls me that." She smiles at that.

"I'm Christabel," she offers. She gives no surname, but I'm not bothered for I didn't give mine either.

"Nice name," I compliment her. Then she asks a question, and it leads to another then another till I find myself having the kind of conversation I've not had since a decade ago when my daughter married and moved out of my house. We talk for a while, until I hear her say she sings for her church choir. Sang, I guess.

"Well, let me hear you sing then?" I ask. She keeps quiet for some time, as if she didn't hear me. Then just when I think she's finally drifted off to sleep, she launches into a song. It is so beautiful that it takes a while for me to realize I've held my breath. As she sings, it's almost as if Death, who was in the room with us, was slowly shrinking away. I find my mind drifting to beautiful things I had not thought of in years. My late wife's musical snoring at night; the time I made enough money to buy my first car... Emotions flood my heart. A single tear strain, or perhaps two, slide down my cheek. She was singing a hymn.

"...whatever my lot, you have taught me to say... It is well ... it is well ...with my soul." I wipe off my tears with the back of my hand as she's about ending.

"That was beautiful," I tell her. But she doesn't respond. *Maybe she's gone back to her sleep.*

The life support machine by her side has not gone off, so I'm not worried. I get up from the chair and grab my mop stick.

"It's Marie," she whispers aloud, "My real name is Marie." "And I'm still Oluu," I say with a smile. Then, I leave.

That was a week ago. Now I stand over her freshly dug grave in my best suit. I occasionally

dab at the tears rolling down my cheek. The funeral is long over. I can't find appropriate words to say.

"It was nice to hear you sing," I mutter.

I turn to walk away, on my way to work. Someone has to mop the corridors where Death often treads. But my mind goes back to Marie, and I say a quiet prayer for her.

Taboos

Fui Can-Tamakloe

Dela tried as much as possible not to make any noise. He found himself in an awkward position, but there was nothing he could do about it. You know how sound travels far in the forest at night.

It was very dark. In fact, the only way he was able to see the two culprits at all was by the reflection of the moon's dim light on the sacred river. Despite his predicament, Dela grinned beside himself with elation. He had finally caught them red-handed. The Chief Priest and his dirty minion, Agbeko. When the other villagers heard what he, Dela, had to tell them, they would change his name from Dela The No-Good Gossip to Dela The Hero. Or Dela The Saviour. He really couldn't decide yet on which one he preferred. So far as the current nickname was changed, he would be happy.

The Chief Priest barked an order and Agbeko waded a little into the waters and pulled on what looked like a fish trap. Dela nearly let out an "Ao!" (something he was prone to doing when he got too excited.) This was better than he had expected! This Chief Priest was a fraud! After going through all those fake rituals to make this river a 'sacred' river not to be touched by any of the fishermen in the village, he himself was fishing in it! Ao, this would make a brilliant story!

—crack—

Dela had stepped on a dry twig, and the sound carried through the forest like that of a canon. Startled by the sound, the Chief Priest looked up.

"Who's there?!" he called out sternly. But the only thing that responded was the rustling of the disturbed bushes, for Dela had wasted no time in running as fast as his short legs would carry him.

"It's probably a bush animal," Agbeko offered, wading back to the bank of the river.

"When I want your opinion, I'll ask for it. Tell me what you saw now."

Agbeko grinned, "First you must tell me I'm your best student. If I hadn't seen this trend we'd ha—"

"One more word from your mouth that isn't in answer to my question and you'll be my only student I sacrificed to Mawu," snarled the Chief Priest.

The grin left Agbeko's face.

"All the fish the trap caught were big. Grown," He answered.

"Good," the Chief Priest smiled, "So maybe we can lift the ban on fishing in this river during the next moon, and then place a ban on the other river. Release the fish and let us go back."

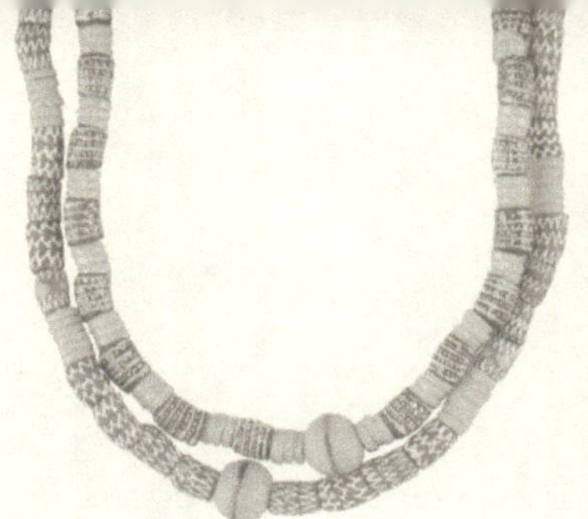

Brave

Gabriella R. Rockson

I'm angry. I've been angry for close to 8 months. Nobody knows—of course—and no one ever has to know. "She was so happy and calm," they'd say. "We can't believe she did that." A tiny giggle escapes my lips. Hiding my smile, I prepare to mingle like the best friend I am. I make small talk and make sure everyone is having a great time as I work my way through the crowd. Smiling and shaking hands, I paint the perfect picture of warmth and friendliness. I'd been studying Devin's mother and I had the act down pat.

Eventually I make eye-contact with the guest of honour, my best friend. He looks so worried. I quickly give him a reassuring smile that says all is forgotten and forgiven. Before I can cross over to join Devin, I'm waylaid by his vapid girlfriend. The last time we met, I felt sorry for her and so sat down with her and listened as she went on and on about her latest worries. She was slightly neurotic and was bordering on irritating. She was only Devin's girlfriend because he felt the need to settle down. Devin's parents—my godparents— were

98

the kind of Ghanaians everyone aspired to be. They were still madly in love. They were down to earth. They were also insanely rich.

Devin was unfortunately the only one who might have known how angry I was. It had happened the previous day. I was testy the whole morning. I see now that I should have had lunch by myself in my room. We had been sitting outside at a small table when he made a careless joke about my scars. I lost it. I turned over the table and slapped him.

Someone else might have thought it normal for me to react that way after what I'd been through. Someone who didn't know how I had acted after the incident. That's what I called it. Right after it happened I had been calm and collected, reassuring anyone who dared to cry about how bad my skin looked. I had smiled and comforted them, letting them know that after my skin graft I'd look brand new. Not once had I yelled or cried. So it was perfectly normal for Devin to think he could make a joke. I was always making jokes about how for someone with such a name, he tended to make crass and very crude statements in the three local languages we spoke.

I fled to my room, locked the door and cried for the first time since my death. That's what I actually called it. Waking up in the hospital and realising what had happened to me had changed me; "Deadened" me. I cried, finally allowing myself to feel the pain I had shut away for so long. I cried until I eventually fell asleep. When I awoke, the first thing I did was to check my phone to see how long I'd slept. Two hours. I had missed 17 calls from Devin. I called him back and we talked. I said what he needed to hear; insulted him as a way of letting him know we were cool, and lay back listening to him talk about the party he was throwing the next day. Yesterday's events would cause me to shift *it* to a further date. There really was no rush.

Making my way across the room, I wondered what people saw when they looked at me. A dark woman wearing a spectacular gown that showed only a glimpse of her neck?

A phenomenal woman who could still socialise despite a horrifying ordeal with her ex- boyfriend who turned out to be a psychopath whose fascination was to inflict multiple cuts on his victims and watch them bleed to death?

Or a woman struggling to appear placid as she plotted how exactly to kill her ex-boyfriend in the most dramatic way possible?

Maybe a Place to Call Home

Gabriella R. Rockson

I absolutely love my new room. It has more things than any room in the old flat had.

"Abena, I hope you like your new room," Ashorkor says brightly, hovering nervously near the door, "We fitted it with things we thought you'd like."

I blink blankly at her, refusing to thank my uncle's wife or offer a benign reply to put her at ease. That would be an insult to my mother. *I need to act like this does not impress me. I can't begin to imagine how angry Mother will be when she comes to get me. They're just going to make everything worse.*

Eventually, Ashorkor leaves the room. I wait to hear the door shut before giving the room a second look. There's a giant bed with pink sheets and pillows that I have to restrain myself from jumping on. The pink isn't a gaudy shade but soft, almost regal looking. The room is painted ocean blue. I also have a desk, which has what looks like a brand-new computer on it.

There's a giant dressing table and a huge walk-in closet. The room is carpeted and has windows that overlook the house garden. After going into my bathroom and looking at the giant shiny bathtub and the shower cubicle, I feel sick.

It is night and I'm sleeping on the carpet without a pillow or cloth and without the air- conditioning turned on. That way, when Mother comes back for me, I'll be able to tell her I hadn't fallen down and kissed the feet of these people who had taken her daughter away from her.

Now, it is morning, and I wake up to see Ashorkor with a slightly angry look on her face. I wait to see if this is the moment where she turns out to be just like Mother; violent whenever she's angry. Half expecting to be hit, I bend my head and look steadily at my lap.

"Abena, we need to talk about your mother." I stiffen and say nothing.

"Look at me when I'm talking to you, Abena," she says firmly.

My eyes fly to Ashorkor's face. My foster-mother-to-be now looks sterner than she'd seemed before.

"I think we're alike, you and I. You see, four years ago, I was married to a different man. We both worked in your Uncle Kojo's office."

I continue to stare blankly at her, betraying no interest in the story she's launched into.

"Senam was the kind of person people took an instant liking to. He was affable and seemed to genuinely care about your well-being. But, he was also an alcoholic who later started beating his wife," she says flatly.

Now, she's telling me about that one time my uncle had seen Senam slap her in the office after work had ended. How Senam had assumed there was no one in the office. How my mother's brother had given him a strong tongue lashing that day and threatened to fire him.

That night, Senam had beaten her with a rage that had terrified her. He had been sober.

"I thought I could handle dealing with his cracks about my weight and ugly face when he was drunk," Ashorkor says, with a pitiful chuckle.

"I thought he'd start therapy or go to rehab and it would all end. I thought that if I worked out a bit more and learnt how to dress up like the other girls in the office, maybe he'd go back to the way he used to be. I thought I could fix him," she says, staring at the carpet as if she could see the past playing out on its surface.

She continues, telling me how she lay there writhing and groaning in pain as the man who was supposed to be her loving husband looked at her with revulsion. He had left the house after that and she had managed to unlock the doors and made a call to Kojo, my uncle. He had taken her to the hospital where she was admitted for a week.

She had waited for her husband to come to the hospital; to come explain why and when she had started to disgust him. She recalls her folly. Only Kojo visited.

She's telling me how she couldn't tell her parents or her friends. How she couldn't explain to them that she had remained in a destructive marriage, harbouring hopes that it would get better. Eventually, she did tell them. In the end, she moved into her parents' house and got a divorce.

Senam agreed to be transferred to one of my uncle's offices in another region if she agreed not to press charges against him. She thought about it for some time but eventually agreed not to press charges.

Ashorkor and my uncle dated for a while. Then they got married. And now, here we were. She gives me a shaky tremulous smile.

"Abena, you have to understand that your mother is not coming back. Your uncle and I are not allowing her anywhere near you. Do you understand? You're safe now; she can't ever hurt you again." She adds softly.

Once again, I stare emptily at her.

Giving me a small smile, she says, "When you decide to, call me Aunty Ashorkor." She gets up.

"I'm going to make breakfast"

"Wait," I mutter before she reaches the door, "I'll help you make breakfast Aunty Ashorkor."

Mama is in The Box

Gabriel Myers Hansen

Mama is in the box. She is wearing a white dress and a chain. They say she is sleeping but when you call her, she doesn't wake up. She doesn't even respond when you shake her.

Yaa doesn't know how to do hair at all! She only knows how to do a ponytail. And she doesn't even know how to do it properly. She doesn't even know how to comb an Afro or tie three balls. She pulls my hair very hard and she says "Sorry, sorry. I won't do it again." But she does it again. Look, look at how loose and crooked she has made my hair. And she has hard palms too. When she touches my forehead, it is like she's scratching it.

I like it better when Mama does my hair. Mama can do the afro and the ponytail far better. Sometimes, she plaits two big horns at the sides of my head and she ties colourful ribbons around them. When she combs my hair, it is painful but not as painful as when Yaa does it. All I have to do is to make a tight fist and the pain will go. As for Yaa, the more I tighten my fist, the more it hurts.

Yaa is our maid. She is tall and fair and very quiet. She doesn't go to school and her English is very bad. She only came to us on weekends to clean the house and wash our clothes. But since Mama became sick, she has come to live with us. She sleeps in the sitting room. She rolls out a mat in the evening when she wants to sleep and in the morning, she folds it and lets it lean it in the corner under the bookshelf beside the small rubber bag. She keeps her clothes in the rubber bag. She cooks the food and boils Mama's herbs. She doesn't eat with us at the dining table; she eats in the kitchen. She sits on a small stool and sets her plate on the floor. Now she does my hair and sometimes, it is she who comes to pick me up from school. Daddy always takes me to school before he goes to work.

Mama doesn't like Yaa anymore; I don't know what she did or why Mama's attitude towards her has changed. Now she calls her "Hɛh" or "Kwɛ". Even when she screams her name from the bedroom, she says "Hɛh Yaa" or "Kwɛ Yaa". Mama says not to call anyone *Aboa*. She says Jesus doesn't like us referring to other people as animals. But when she's angry at Yaa, she eyes her and calls her *aboa*. When Yaa says good morning, Mama doesn't respond, she only waves her left hand at her. Sometimes, I watch her when she cries in the kitchen but she doesn't know that I'm watching her. One day, I asked her why she was crying and she said that she wasn't crying. She wiped her face with the dirty wrapper she had on her waist and smiled.

But Daddy likes Yaa very much. He smiles and says good morning when Yaa greets. He also asks, "How are you doing?" When he returns, he asks her if she has eaten and sometimes he buys her gifts. You see the red blouse Yaa wears now to the market? It was Daddy who bought it for her. Her new sandals too, it was Daddy who bought them. When Daddy gives Yaa something new, she says, "Thank you Daddy. Thank you very much. May God bless you, Daddy". Daddy is not her father but she calls him Daddy. Her Mama and Daddy live in the village. Daddy said we might visit them this December. I can't wait.

As soon as I get home from school,, I run to the bedroom to greet Mama. Sometimes, she's asleep but I shake her and she wakes up. I sing the songs Auntie Rhoda taught at school that day. She helps me with my homework. She says I'm clever and she wants me to become a lawyer. But I want to become a doctor.

I want to wear a white coat and inject people. I wanted to be a teacher before, like Auntie Rhoda. I wanted to lash all the bad boys who sit at the back and disturb and bully, like Attoh Graham and Quaye Michael. But the last time Daddy and I took Mama to the hospital and I saw a doctor wearing glasses and something around his neck, I just wanted to be a doctor.

Mama knows all the rhymes Auntie Rhoda teaches us so she sings along. Mama can sing oh, she can sing very well. Yaa too can sing, but she doesn't know rhymes.

Do you know Auntie Fofo? She's the best aunt in the world. She visits us often, especially since Mama's sickness. She brings fruits and herbs for Mama and biscuits for me. Sometimes she brings biscuits for Yaa too. She has big eyes and big cheeks. She's fat, but not *obolo*. I like her car very much. It's a Benz. I'll buy one when I grow up. I love her very much. She calls Daddy "Ken" and calls Mama "Adoley".

On the day of the funeral, Auntie Fofo asked me, "Where is Mama?" and I said, "Mama is in the box." Then she was smiling but tears were flowing from her eyes. She pulled me to her chest and hugged me tightly. I asked her why she was crying and she said she was not crying. I also began to cry and she told me to stop crying but she was still crying.

Tears Don't Last

Hakeem Adam

Now, the reader should be able to observe an iconic group of kids in visibly dirty, loose hanging, tattered clothes. The clothes are like billboards, advertising the state of deprivation and decay in which the wearers exist. From this, it is clear the kids are in no satellite-dish neighbourhood with manicured lawns, sprinkler systems, guard dogs and tinted sedans. No. The kids are a few steps from an uncovered drain, or better still, gutter (accurately capturing the gut-content-like material stagnated in it). A vendor is in her element, dishing "Special Waakye" to a winding queue of exuberant patrons; you would think they had lined up at the gates of heaven.

Across the street lies the subject of one of the boys' rooted attention. Over the granite and coal tar sits a shipping container painted blue, with the label "Dons Game Centre" stencilled in blood red across it. British football commentary is blaring from the subwoofer in the container. The boy easily recognizes the voice of Martin Tyler. The front of the container is screened with what appears to be a flour sack, once white but now something between dark brown and black, obviously transformed by the filthy hands that molest it constantly. A man in a Chelsea FC jersey, wearing a rugged *thugged-out* look, sits in front of the sack with a long, thin cane in one hand.

The boy is staring at the man, who visibly has cold salty tears seeping from the corners of his coloured eyes. His torso trembles with every weighted breath. The reader should discern that he is in great pain.

Had the reader joined the scene a few minutes earlier, she would have observed that same crying child kneeling in front of the container, with the man dropping saliva and insults on his ringworm infested head. Then after, the boy being dragged to his feet and beaten like a warning drum. The boy, itching to be free of the pain, in a failed ploy to dodge the strokes, pivots around the man, with his shorts in the hand of his molester being the fixed point. The man, who appears to be satisfied after a while, hurls the boy onto the street.

The boy begins to yell a name frantically in the direction of the container, but the sub-woofer drowns out his voice. It appears he is calling a friend who is still in the container. The rest of the boys in the group cannot be seen in the scene now. He is the only one left near the "Special Waakye".

A young woman carrying an ice chest on her not so pleasant-smelling weave-on walks by, swaying her hips as she screams;" Yess, Brukinaaa!" She seems to seize the attention of the man in front of the container. He calls her and proceeds to buy from her. After opening the bottle and gulping a quarter down, he begins to pat his pocket for money to pay the woman. The intensity and speed with which he performs the action begins to increase, as if his pants were on fire. It is with wide-eyed, open-mouthed shock that he realizes he has been robbed.

The boy, upon noticing this, wipes his tears on his forearm, cracks a foxy smile from the corner of his lips and begins to scurry away.

The Wedding People

Hakeem Adam

You all should know that Aunty K has an abominable character. She is an exquisite Machiavellian renowned for setting small fires in different parts of the home and watching her inferno grow from a distance and engulf her 'loved ones'. Now that she has moved away from us, I can speak freely. She is truly an enigma. Let me guide you through her story.

You should notice her clearly, right there, with the big black handbag and signature sinister look; arched eyebrows, squinted eyes and pouted mouth. Aside the obvious, she blends in perfectly with the rest of the crowd at the wedding—All smiles, laughs and the usual comments and questions; "I've not seen you since you were a little baby!", "Look how tall you have grown!", "Do you remember me?"

Whilst everyone else is as actively involved as people at a Ghanaian wedding ought to be, Aunty K has tasked herself with repossessing her donation.

"Hurry up! Keep them coming. I saw some boxes of Jack Daniels and Moet in the room. Try to get those. And don't get caught." She barks at her twelve-year-old son who does not understand why his mother needs all that booze and why he must use the kitchen door to stay out of sight as much as possible.

"Foolish people! Upon all the money you have, you want me to contribute to your wedding, buy *Gele*, and do *Buki*. Habaa! What did they ever do for me? That my foolish brother, when I wanted money to go to Dubai, you said the economy. But the economy gave you a new Benz. Now you want me to contribute to your disrespectful daughter's wedding."

She convinces herself of her purpose whilst arranging the bottles in her bag, and ends the monologue with a long dragging chuckle that is conveniently drowned by the *Kora* and Calabash ensemble.

As the day begins to lose its youth, the wedding party gets bigger. Aunty K, who has more than replenished her donation, decides to leave. She asks her son, Iddi, "the courier" to take her much bigger bag to the car, specifically saying: "Take it to the car. I will hold the small one. If anyone asks you, say it is not for me. It is for the wedding people."

She holds the tip of her earlobe firmly and warns, "Have you heard?"

Iddi, not surprised by his mother's compulsive lying; nods like an agama lizard and sets about discharging his task.

Aunty K gets home late and is too tired to check her goods. She goes straight to bed and falls into a very deep sleep. She is awoken the next day, just after midday, by a very unwelcome phone call. It is her newly wedded niece.

"Aunty K, how are you? I hope I am not disturbing you?"

"Oh my dear, I am very well. How is married life treating you?"

"Haha, oh, Aunty K, I am also alright. We saw your many gifts and we just wanted to say a big thank you. We were a bit surprised that they were all bottles of very expensive alcohol. You know we don't drink, but anyway, thank you very much. They will make for nice decorations. No one gave us as many gift as you did. I am touched by this…"

As soon as she hangs up the phone, Aunty K's head begins to swirl. She yells out for Iddi. "Iddi, what happened to the black bag last night?"

"Mommy, I was sending it but I didn't know where you parked the car. I was looking around when Uncle and his people asked me what was in the bag. I said I did not know, but it was for the wedding people. So they took it and said they knew where to put it."

Edɔ

Ivana Akotowaa Ofori

Maya had been my best friend since Primary 6. That meant seventeen years of friendship. Apart from a few quickly-resolved arguments, we got along swimmingly, even to the extent of having a double wedding last year—she to her man, Kwaku, and me to mine, Aaron. Maya had always been an amazing, steadfast friend. I couldn't ask for anyone better.

There was just one thing… it irked me time and time again: Maya criticized my food all the time; not what I ate, but what I cooked. Every time she came over and I made any local meal for her, she'd snidely comment, "Ah, Shika! As for this one, it's like there's no pepper inside. Ei! Are you sure you are Ga?"

What audacity! What right had she to judge my meals, when I made them just the way I wanted to eat them? And for as long as we had known each other, even before we'd gotten married, Aaron had never had a problem with the hotness of my food or denounced me from the ethnic group we both belonged to.

I soon discovered it wasn't just me Maya did this to. Our mutual friend, Serwaa, complained to me about it frequently, then we vented our frustrations together, only to allow it to occur *again*… Until, one day, a wicked idea occurred to me. Devoid of premature guilt, I carried it out four days later.

I told Serwaa to tell Maya to come over so we could all go and pick up my sister from the airport at twelve. Both of them were friends with my sister so it wasn't a hard ask.

At nine, I made my way to the little stall I used to visit so frequently. The shopkeeper, whom I'd only ever known as Maame, exclaimed in Ga, "Shika! Long time no see. Ever since you started making your own shito, you won't even come and greet me."

"Oh, Maame, you see, it's the work and the husband keeping me busy. Anyway…how much is the hottest shito you have?"

Maame looked absolutely startled. She knew for a fact I couldn't eat hot shito. In all my years of shopping from her. I'd never bought any jar of shito beyond the "mild" label. Yet, here I was, inquiring about very, very hot shito—the one that only the sixty-something-year-old Ga men bought—the ones who believed they had bowels of stone; it was the shito they ate to prove they were men.

Maame recovered quickly enough. She handed me the pepper. I handed her the cash and returned home to cook. As soon as I was done, the gate bell rang. *Go-time.*

"Oh, you guys," I told Serwaa and Maya remorsefully, "The airport gave me the wrong time! The flight is landing at three, not twelve."

This, of course, was no news to Serwaa. Maya, on the other hand, was highly irritated. "Three!" she exclaimed. "You can't be serious. I don't have time to go back home. Do you have food? Because I'm broke and I'd rather not starve."

I smiled. "Don't worry. I just finished frying some delicious yam. All of you are invited."

Four plates. Each stacked with spear-like, golden-yellow slices of hot, fried yam. Each with a side of sardine and homemade shito.

The plan almost failed: as Maya reached for the first plate, I quickly snatched it away, saying how I'd better save it for Aaron, and placed it in the microwave. She was forced to take another, completely unsuspecting. I didn't object.

We sat down in front of the TV, watching some very early rerun of *Hangin' With Mr. Cooper*. Two minutes into the meal, Maya started to breathe through her mouth. Three minutes later, she began to sweat profusely. I knew her—she was too proud to ask for water.

Serwaa innocently volunteered to switch on the air-conditioner. The sweating receded. The heavy breathing did not.

Serwaa and I ate hungrily, practically licking our plates clean. Maya's remained over half- full. It looked as if her tongue would no longer fit in her mouth. Her forehead was glistening with large droplets. You could hear her panting like a thirsty dog all the way across the room.

Maybe it was a mean trick, but so far, she hadn't said a single derogatory word about my shito—even if she had, it would have been invalid, because she wasn't eating *my* shito.

"Shika, your shito really rocked today. Maya, how are you finding it?" asked Serwaa.

"Maya!" I said, pretending to have just noticed her condition. "Did you take a splash in a fountain or something? What's wrong with you?"

Maya swallowed, opened her mouth and tried to suppress a gasp. She failed. Her eyes were watering. "The pepper is hot," she whispered.

"What's that?" I inquired. "I couldn't quite catch that."

"I said," she almost yelled, "the shito is hot! God, it's too hot!"

"Too hot?!" I repeated incredulously. "I made you your own separate shito, you know? I always got the impression my regular one was too mild for you. I thought you'd enjoy this."

Maya stared at me, pained. "No…" She didn't get any further before she had to rush out of the room to get a glass of water.

This was the day. I had won. I had finally won. Maya would never be able to insult my pepper again. I gave Serwaa a sneaky high five and revelled in my triumph.

Maya came back, face washed, thirst quenched and, I supposed, most of the burning gone too. She sat down and said: "Shika, you're always getting it wrong. Either your pepper has no sting at all, or it's too hot it has no flavour. If you like, I can teach you how I make my own."

I slumped back in my chair, thinking "*You have got to be kidding me!*"

Mango

Ivana Akotowaa Ofori

There were three of us; the squad—Etornam, Delasie and myself, Yao. We had been friends practically since birth. Quite recently, I had taken a special liking to Delasie. So had Etornam. While I had noticed his attraction to her and he had noticed mine, we never said a word about it to each other, or her. It was a silent conundrum of agreed solidarity.

Delasie was a very attractive female with an enticing personality and the strange ability to get most males to do whatever she wanted. Unfortunately for Etornam and I, this meant that we were not her only suitors—but we had grown so comfortable with our game that we couldn't bear to have the delicate balance tipped by another boy.

His name was Edem, but everyone called him Mottoway. It was a corruption of 'motorway', because he had this huge gap between his front incisors, and the running joke was that it was so wide, it could be used as a motorway for trucks. He was younger than us, and like many others, hopelessly devoted to Delasie.

He was constantly hovering over us, greeting, "Fine day, Sister Dela," on the way to school; greeting only her, as if Etornam and I weren't even there. Each time he got the opportunity, he was asking if there was anything he could provide for "Sister Dela", be it fetching her water, helping her cross the line to the latrine or cutting open her coconut.

Eventually, I got fed up of Mottoway, and convened with Etornam in line with our unspoken agreement that we were the only ones allowed to chase after Delasie. Together, we came up with a plan. Delasie gladly agreed to help.

The next day, pretending to be taking a leisurely walk, we passed right in front of Mottoway's house at a time we knew he would be outside. He came rushing with that daft, helpless look of his on his face.

"Is there anything I can do for you, Sister Dela?" "Actually, yes," she replied.

Mottoway's eyes lit up with eagerness and blind devotion. "Oh, just say it, sister, I promise I will get it for you!"

Delasie turned on the honeyed voice and flirtatious looks she always gave to boys when she wanted something done for her. "I want a mango. But not just any mango from anywhere! I want a mango from the top of the tallest mango tree in the area. The one behind Aunty Dorothy's house."

"Err…yes sister. But—" He was starting to look worried. "But Sister Dela, it's tall oh! Are you sure you want the mango from that tree?" He wouldn't even consider how strange it was that she only wanted a mango from *one* particular tree, but he was worried about its height. How daft!

Delasie sighed. "If you're scared, it's okay. I'll just ask Yao or Etornam to get it for me."

He was horrified at the prospect. "No need for that, Sister! I can do it. In fact, I will bring the mango to your house in one hour."

Twenty minutes later, we were all hiding a safe distance away, watching Mottoway's attempts to climb the mango tree.

"Ah," complained Etornam. "So he still won't give up?"

Mottoway finally got up on the branch that had been impeding his ascent for a while. We were all astonished. From there, it wouldn't be very hard to get further up and find a good mango.

"My goodness, he's actually doing it!" whispered Delasie.

As we watched, he got to the top, and then froze. I barely noticed; I was still very much irritated at the fact that our trick had failed and he'd been able to perform the stupid, dangerous task instead of wallow and weep in the realisation that he'd never win Delasie's heart.

A few minutes later, he was still at the top of the tree, not having moved any more than six inches. Then it dawned on me: the boy had serious vertigo! He must be terrified of heights!

"Yao, what do we do? Oh, Etornam, how can we get him down?" Delasie nearly cried. She felt guilty for agreeing to our plan. But why should she blame herself for someone else being in love and doing stupid things?

I emerged from our hiding place and walked over to the tree. "Edem! Hurry up and come down!" I yelled.
"I can't!" he screamed back. He was in tears.

"Don't be an idiot!" I said. "Come down before I come up there myself and lash you! Foolish boy! If you know you cannot come down from the tree, why did you climb it?"

I was putting on this display of bravado both to disguise my own anxiety. I thought I could bully him into letting his inherent defiance and boyish pride get to his head and save him. It was of no use. He only cried harder. I was beginning to think that was hopeless—that there was no way to get him down, when I heard Delasie approach me. Her expression had changed entirely from frightened and helpless to stern and no-nonsense.

"Edem," she said slowly, steadily and deliberately. "You will come down right now and stop this foolishness. All this for one mango? Please. Carry it in your teeth and climb back down."

That was all it took. Mottoway obeyed to the last word, and soon, he was down with us.

How did she *always* do it? This power of command over males simply wasn't natural. That was the first time I began to suspect that Delasie was an actual witch.

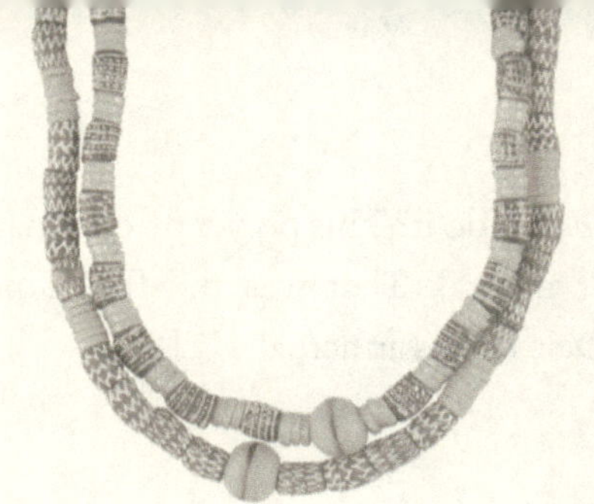

All in a Night's Work

Jermaine Kudiabor

Innocence breathed deeply. He tugged his black jacket closer around his shoulders. It was a chilly night. There was a full moon, and it provided the only light along the tarred road. The street-lights had long been destroyed by the wayside robbers who prowled this route. Every few minutes, a taxi would roar by, its headlights making it look like some amber-eyed monster. The bush on one side of the road was filled with the music of crickets, and the occasional sound of some creepy-crawly thing moving within the undergrowth. This was the perfect scene for a horror movie, or a mugging.

"Hey you", a voice boomed. "You know the way to New Ejisu?"

Innocence looked towards the bush and had his view almost fully obstructed by a massive chest in a black and white striped muscle shirt. Innocence was no wimp, but this guy reminded him of WWE matches between Great Khali and Rey Mysterio. He could smell the heavy scent of weed in the air. The figure stepped into the moonlight and Innocence, much against his own will, gulped. The guy's dark, hard face had a long scar from the right side of his forehead to his cheek. His red eyes quickly went over Innocence's jacket and black knapsack, his Tag Heuer gold watch, and moved down to the black Levis and expensive Nike he had on. A sly looking grin twisted his already dangerous looking features.

"You'd have to walk along the road till you get to the crossroad junction, then you turn right." Innocence croaked.

"Since you seem to be going there I hope you don't mind if I tag along?" the smile appeared again, the scariest attempt at affability he'd ever seen. Innocence couldn't say no, so they set off together. The giant took his time walking, and Innocence had to shorten his stride to accommodate him. His name was Gideon, but everyone called him "Shotta", he said. He asked for Innocence's name, and where he lived. He added that he was from the nearby nightclub and had gotten lost on his way home. Innocence was the only one he'd seen that night. That last statement put him at rest somewhat, but he still didn't let his eyes off the huge man. Was it a trick of the moonlight, or did he see a grin when he told Shotta he didn't stay anywhere around here? "Don't move!" Shotta barked.

Innocence froze, just as he asked. The moon had chosen this time to hide her face in a cloud, as if terrified of what was to come. Even the crickets in the bush had gone silent. They were alone. The blow to his head wasn't hard enough to knock him out, but he still saw stars as he fell to the ground.

"That's so you don't have any funny ideas. Give me your watch and everything else before this becomes more painful for you." A kick in the ribs made Innocence grunt in pain.

"Please, I beg", Innocence said weakly as huge hands grabbed him by his jacket and hauled him to his feet.

Innocence let the jack knife he'd palmed as he lay on the cold road slash across the man's throat. Shotta stepped back as his blood started to trickle down his neck like a waterfall of wine, his eyes opened in shock. Innocence followed his step, plunging his knife into his chest over and over again, even as the man lay still on the road. He knelt by the thug, his arms shaking and breathing hard with exhaustion, but with a maniacal grin on his face. He ripped open the man's shirt and placed the tip of the knife under his left breast, and pushed downwards…

Innocence was covered in blood after he was done cutting out the heart and testicles. He took out the spare clothes in his knapsack and changed, wiping the blood carefully off him. With his soiled clothes, he wrapped the body parts the fetish priest had requested for the money ritual and carefully shoved it into his bag. He dragged the body into the bush and continued walking along the road to New Ejisu.

The moon had glided back into view now. He could see better with its light. He tried to whistle an accompaniment to the crickets' symphony, and there was a spring in his step as he walked, his sneakers crunching on the gravel.

Room 22

Jermaine Kudiabor

Beeeep beeeeep. Beeeep beeeeep.
"Yo Kofi, what's up?" "TK. I dey"
There was silence after Kofi's voice echoed oddly on the line.
"You no dey play FIFA?"
"Nah, not today."

TK lived for FIFA tournaments. I used to join him every Friday. But I just didn't understand how anyone could stick to one game for ever. I mean, *there's Call of Duty*!

"One of these days I for come school you then your guys. The way I upgrade…"

"Hoh. Wey upgrade? You no for come here sef. Just call me make I come own you then your squad. You no dey play proper games…"

Our banter continued till TK asked, "How's Keli?"

I took a swig from the beer can I'd instinctively taken from the six pack and mumbled nervously.

"We split. New guy and stuff"

"Slow. New guy? He better than you?"

"She wants him more. Besides, I hit it so whoever he is, he's entitled to my leftovers."

I wish I meant that remark. I honoured that girl more than I honoured my father and mother.

Forgive me Lord.

"You sure? You swore she was the one."

"We all make mistakes man. I just got over mine." "Man, I dunno, if Shasha left me I'd just die, man."

"Hahaha! Lover boy TK. The way you take this girl hide me dierr, you really cherish her… but trust me, you'll get over it if it happens. Anyway, look, I was just calling to ask what's up."

"Oh, cool. Thanks, man. You know, we should get together real quick and talk. Catch up
on old times and stuff."

"Yeah… that'll be nice. Dude, gotta go. I'll see you real soon" I said. "Sure thing man. Later."

"Safe" I said, and cut the call.

I pulled the glove box open and took out the photograph of TK, with my Kekeli. A friend had taken this picture two days ago. It hadn't taken long to find out which cheap motel they were staying at. Underneath the picture was a suppressed pistol. I didn't even know what calibre or model it was. All I knew was that if I pointed and squeezed the trigger, it would do the job for me. I slid it carefully under my belt and downed the rest of the beer. Then I got out of my car and walked towards the motel.

There was practically no security, just a drunk guard who would not remember my face. I walked in and stood in front of Room 22. This was where they were. They were probably fucking right now. I wondered if I should knock and have one of them open up. No, this would be better. I aimed at the lock.

TK hung up and turned to Keli.

"You know he'll find out sooner or later, right?" "It doesn't matter. He can't do anything about it".

"Yeah, but he's my friend. He was trying to act tough, but I know Kofi. He's always been a soft guy."

She snorted, "Leftovers? That idiot wasn't man enough to touch me. Kept talking about the right time. He was so boring, not like you. I love you," She wrapped her arms around TK and started trailing kisses across his broad chest till he grabbed her chin and pulled her lips upward.

They were like that when the first shots fired.

Maame Abena's Visitor

Jesse Jojo Johnson

Saturday 12th June, nine in the evening. The third day.

Three hours after the rain, the frogs outside are still at it. She chooses to stay in her room and drown in the incessant chorus. She is huddled in a corner of her bed, chin rested on her knees as she rocks from side to side. She stares at the night through the window that overlooks the garden—or what is left of it after grandma, its sole tender, died.

The weeds thrive in the wake of her demise. The rains, seeing there is no one left to worry about those delicate rose stems, have carried them away, along with the rich black soil and even some of the underlying clay. Everything has been washed down into the gutter in front of the house—the one that drains the cesspit.

Harriet must have loved seeing the evidence of the old lady's industriousness and craft. Anytime she woke up, she would spend five minutes of her quiet time contemplating the dew-drenched soil, the mixture of petals bathed in the morning, the heaviness of dawn, before she picked her Bible for the day's devotion.

That Bible is under her pillow. It hasn't come out in three weeks.

Three weeks ago, mother dragged father out of bed. It was past midnight, but Harriet was still awake. What was she doing? Listening? There were phone calls. Mother's shadow could be seen from the glowing threshold, crisscrossing the corridor, her footsteps muffled by the carpet. Father, he wanted sleep, but his wife's mother was in critical condition. They left thirty minutes later.

Father returned alone. Harriet had just finished her quiet time, but something told her not to go out and greet him. "I'll stay in my room and wait for him to tell me." she decided, and coiled herself under her covers. Dawn turned to daylight and the sun spread across her room. It must have been seven, or eight. She was hungry. She was scared.

Father didn't check up on her until noon. She must have dozed off because one moment she was tracing circles in her pillow, the next he was seated on her bed, back against the wall, blocking the sunlight. He cast a shadow across her face. His silhouette against the window frame was slumped. He hadn't slept well.

"Harriet", his voice was froggy. He offered a hand. She took it and drew herself from under her covers. He held her to his chest. Then she cried.

Awo had nine children. Her three eldest sons lived in the UK and couldn't make it on such short notice; something about work and family and the airfare. That was okay. They sent money for the funeral.

Mother had to house her two brothers and two sisters. Her older sister had died before Harriet was born. "It's only death that will bring us together. Look at the mess we've become!" she kept repeating after thirty minutes on various phone calls.

Harriet's uncles and aunts came in on Monday night. Mother recited their names to her when they arrived but Harriet, poor child, she couldn't keep the litany in her head. It wasn't mother's fault that she didn't know them better. They blamed Awo for that too.

The final rites were to take place on the third week after Awo's death. The house was full of strange voices and new scents. Harriet didn't talk much during those final days. A lot of old people came in and went out. Most of the time, the sitting room was prepared for guests. There was always alcohol for the grownups and malt for their children. So many conversations, laughing, weeping, consoling. The change kept Harriet in her room, locked up and contemplating the garden just as Awo had left it. She could do nothing but watch the house, the patch of black, petal strewn earth, the whole world transform around her.

Saturday 12th June, nine-thirty in the evening. The third day. Amid the unabated croaking outside, Harriet hears her name. "Maame Abena". It comes from outside.

She had said she would always be outside. "Maame Abena, did you brush your teeth tonight?"

"Grandma there are plenty people in the house! I can't go out!"

"Ah! Herh, Maame, will they eat you?" "No, but I don't like them!"

"Hmm! You think I like them? Look, Maame they are my children. They are harmless." "Okay, Grandma", comes her emphatic concession.

"So, after this will you go and brush your teeth?" Harriet nods. "Good! Don't forget to pray, okay?"

"Grandma, I want to pray to God that I will see you soon." She speaks a little too loudly. A shadow crossing the threshold stops.

Awo puts a finger across her lips and looks at the poor child with a stern eye. Harriet smiles back.

The shadow goes its way. The conversation resumes in whispers. "Maame, so you haven't pulled the weeds like I asked you to?"

"Oh, Grandma! I'm sorry. The people said they will leave tomorrow. They said there will be thanksgiving and then they will leave. Then I can go out and clean the garden."

Awo feigns doubt and disappointment. It gets to Harriet. It always does. The old lady laughs at her granddaughter.

"Oh, Grandma..." but Awo has to leave.

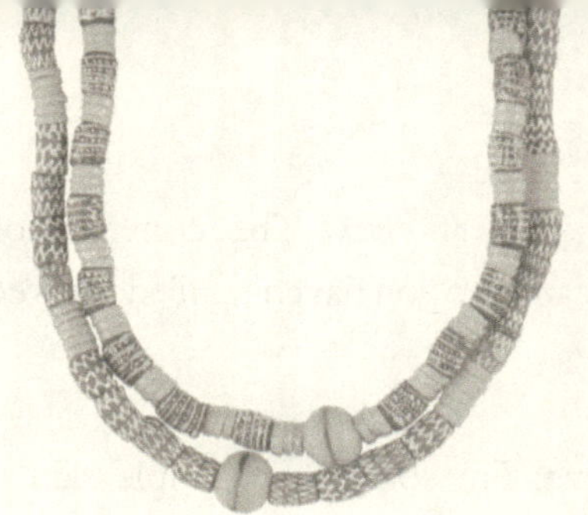

Mr. Adamafio's Problem

Jesse Jojo Johnson

Before Doctor Adamu turned to his next patient, he frowned at the tables on his monitor. He entered another search term, and the result set came cascading down in needless, showy animation. He scoffed. "We paid five thousand cedis for cartoons", then he scrolled furiously down, scanning an average of ten lines per second, until his brain recognized a pattern and froze every muscle in his right hand.

He picked up the hospital card and cross-checked her name: *Patricia Fuseina Agyeman.* He grunted something under his breath and narrowed into her entry.

"Trauma from third incident with husband. Religious differences taking toll on subject. Triggered by the name of Christ, among other ritual symbols."

He hit [Enter] like it was a recalcitrant child.

"Trauma from stillbirth. Religious interpretation of medical issues leading to distorted perception. Investigate verbal, physical abuse. Detain."

He saved her file and slid the hospital card beneath a pile in a drawer to his left, then he spun his seat to face the sullen gentleman, placed crossed hands authoritatively in front of him and cracked open a smile.

"How are you?" his voice was the voice of God: it came from a place of authority, grounded in the unshakable truths that sat at the foundation of scientific progress.

Doctor Adamu was a bastion of knowledge and goodwill, a fountain of modern virtue built on the minds of great men of medicine he studied night and day. From his bounty, he dispensed healing to a broken world.

Mr. Adamafio shifted his feet. He was not on good terms with the chair, choosing to sit at the very edge and refusing entirely to be comfortable. He refused to raise his head. The room was cold. He rubbed his arms for warmth.

"Fine", his words were heavy laden. He could not look into the face of the man who would help him with his illness. Doctor Adamu knew this sort. He only smiled.

"What is your name?" the doctor asked his patient, while reading through his file. *35-year- old man. Newly married.* He needed to start a conversation, and this sort was in no mood for that.

Mr. Adamafio stretched a trembling finger toward the doctor and pointed to the card he was holding. "There" he whispered to no one in particular.

This time Doctor Adamu *really* smiled. He must be intelligent. So, what is the meaning of this?

"How is your wife?" the doctor asked, trying to breach the stronghold. His patient shrugged and shook his head at the same time. *"No, I don't know."* That is what he meant.

Or was it *"I don't know. Not good."*? Perhaps.

Doctor Adamu nodded to himself, and scribbled something on an A4 sheet. He turned it so Mr. Adamafio wouldn't read it. Though his patient was downcast, the rapid movement of his eyes was apparent through his eyelids.

"Smart man", Doctor Adamu reminded himself. He reclined in his seat and let it creak until he was satisfied. *"He's avoidant. We can't have a reasonable conversation. He won't open up. Look at his eyes. He's taking in a lot of information"*.

He watched as the silence relaxed Mr. Adamafio's breathing.

"If I give him time he'll rationalise his way out of this. He's settling. He's trying to assess the situation so he can adjus—"

"What is wrong with you?!" the doctor shot at him like a mad man: there was a dark glimmer in his eyes. His hands, like claws, trapped the poor man's hands where they rested on his desk.

Mr. Adamafio squirmed at the edge of his seat. He had nowhere to hide. His hands were caught in the snare.

Now that his prey was left open, Doctor Adamu was ruthless. He knew he could not reason with a determined mad man. He must shock him out of his prison. "Mr. Adamafio," he barked into his face, each syllable lashing the stricken man.

"What is the matter, sir? I want you to tell me everything." And so his gaze was fixed on his patient's eyes. They were red and swollen. His lips trembled with words that wanted freedom. His face was blackened by his misfortune, disfigured by his mental agony.

"My wife..."

"What did she do to you?" the doctor urged him like a father, leaning closer, breathing into his face.

Mr. Adamafio was shaking his head, letting a pathetic "No" escape in unsure gasps.

"Okay. Sorry. What did you do to your wife?" The patient flinched at that reconstruction, but Doctor Adamu kept his hold on him. Then he smiled and nodded.

"My wife...I..." Mr. Adamafio was stuttering. He seemed to grow faint, nodding gently towards the doctor. He was soaking his Vodafone t-shirt with sweat. Even in the cold air-conditioned room.

"I have worked mischief between her thighs!" He blurted and snapped free from his doctor's grasp.

The old man fell back from the shock, caught his mouth open and shut it. He adjusted his glasses and regained composure. He was not sure of what he had heard.

Mr. Adamafio wasn't sure either. The words had rebelled against him and come out of their own will. They did not even use his voice. It was not him.

Yet it was him. His breathing, erstwhile frantic, began to fall to a gentler rhythm. His lips were pursed, as if to keep more confessions from embarrassing him. He looked at Doctor Adamu from beneath furious brows. Doctor Adamu stared back.

"You slept with your wife?" "Yes."
"And?"

Mr. Adamafio nodded.

"Did you rape her?" He shook his head.

"Was it entirely consensual?" by this time the doctor was scribbling on his sheet. The patient's wandering eyes caught him. He placed a hand on his writing.

"How long ago was this?" "Three days."
"Your first time?" "Yes."

Virgin. Middle aged. Acute anxiety. Guilt and regret. Conflicted conscience. Doctor Adamu was putting down the clues. He stopped. He shook his head, raised his eyebrows as the puzzle pieces fell in perfect place.

"What church do you go to?" "Saint Francis..."
Repressed.

Doctor Adamu leaned back in his seat and looked at the man. He was haggard. His pained expression still remained after the revelation. He could not look up at the doctor. Perhaps he was embarrassed, but this was a problem. It was the source of all problems. Doctor Adamu clasped his hands round his mouth and breathed warmth into his palms. He was tossing things in his mind.

Slowly, he leaned forward and entered another search query into the database. He typed it out slowly. His chest was still pounding from the exchange. He could hear the pulse in his ears. The result set cascaded down. It was a smaller set.

Reginald Adamafio. He found the record.

Post-coital anxiety. Acute. Long time virgin. Well educated. Likely repressed/ suffering from suppressed trauma. Detain.

He hit [Enter].

Sunset Bar

Jesse Jojo Johnson

The half empty glass stood before Isaac like a philosophical issue worth investigating. He interrogated it with his eyes, noting how it distorted the red sunset like a tongue of fire splashing towards him, painting the mahogany coloured counter.

For a moment, everything about him was muted. The universe became his mind and the kaleidoscope of colours dancing in front of him: symptoms of the life he had ostracised. For a moment only.

Then, like the shock of cold water on a harmattan morning, memory rich in detail washed over him. He shuddered as the fins of the air conditioner directed an uncouth blast of wind over his shoulder, biting into his coat. He tasted blood inside his cheek.

His hands, heavy as lead, moved as though they were burdened with all the cares in this world towards the fire. It was a long journey. Words took shape in his ears, refusing to be let out of his mind. From memory or from the bar, he could not tell. His gaze shifted in and out of focus; one moment a cold glass, another a burning coal—

—until his fingers reached it and dispelled the illusion. He clasped the glass and brought it home. It burned a good sort of burning. After that, he was himself.

Isaac sighed and turned towards the bartender. He didn't want to: his mind compelled him to keep up the appearance but his feigned disgust was outdone by simple human curiosity and so, unwilling as he was, he turned to his right to see whose smell had claimed his attention.

It was biting and female, dangerous and sensual in the right proportions: a cocktail of flavour that at once revolted and enticed him. He turned a greater angle to catch a better glimpse. A dash of oversaturated red burned the side of his head and ignited interest. Her laughter had a rich, wooden tone, like a low register string.

She settled on the seat, her back at an angle to him. She put her phone on the counter and adjusted the stool under her ample cheeks. The bartender brought her a glass of dark red. She let the wine touch her lips, then she coolly set it down, reached into her bag for a card and delicately lifted her phone.

There were marks where her wedding ring had come off—a deeper dent near the top, suggesting some gem stone. Some of her brown nail polish had brushed the cuticle of the same finger. Her thumbnail was chipped at a corner.

8-0-2-4

She unlocked her phone. Multiple unread messages from *HOPSAN-'08*, and *Richmond. Darling* was still typing...

Enough! He shrunk from all he allowed himself to see. The air conditioner sighed his way again. He shuddered inside his thick coat.

Heat. He fumbled for the glass. Tipped it into his mouth, then reached with his tongue to scrape the remnants of spirit before it was all lost. He slammed it down, and grunted audibly as though something was visibly wrong.

For an uncomfortable moment, he was naked, and all those eyes, a thousand and one of them watched and wondered at him. Even the woman in red with the iPhone and the messages from all those people. She must have looked his way and wondered what on earth a man was doing here alone, shaken like an afflicted child.

He almost cowered under their weight but then, as if it were a joke, collected himself just in time.

The door swung open again but admitted no strangers into the bar. Abigail still had that purple dress with the tie & dye hem badly stitched on by her failed-schoolmate-turned- seamstress.

And she still wore those brown slippers that rattled him whenever he saw them in front of the toilet door. She still had that lazy walk, her shoulders were hunched forward. Her feet looked in opposite directions and her new fiancé had not yet managed to wipe off her foolish grin.

Her fiancé gingerly closed the door gently behind her and skipped lightly to find a suitable spot. She stood there like a dunce while the lanky clerk took a table for two in the far corner of the bar, just beside the window so he had a view of traffic on the 37 Military Hospital Road.

He wiped the seat with a black hanky and dusted the table with more vigour than was necessary. He motioned for her to come. She waddled towards him. She hadn't stopped that.

Whatever made a man love a woman? He asked, but found no strength for philosophising himself out of the mood. He allowed the thoughts to take him deeper. He fingered the rim of the glass and paid no attention to whatever else was going on. Only Abigail and Dave.

Dave GodIsMyRefuge Ahiable. It was a stupid name, but he had it burned in his mind, along with her name and the updated relationship status. He tried to check himself, but deep within, Isaac yearned to wallow like a pig in the shit of his thoughts.

Dave had liked every profile picture she had uploaded since 2011. He would randomly comment "Ma angel!", "u a goldn flower drop 4rm heaven #loveu#", each comment was marked with a solitary *Like*.

He'd smile to himself and remind the new guy telepathically that he had banged the sense out of this one since their university days. One Down's afflicted baby and those aborted twins later, he'd had it. He'd sent her an SMS from Aburi. He was taking the weekend off. He was bored. He didn't wish to see her when he returned.

Like the simple girl she was, not a trace of her existence remained when he got back home a week later. "Maybe she went to her mother", he reasoned as he basked in the silence of his hard-won freedom.

He had asserted himself over society by taking apart what had been put together. This was the first triumph in his endeavour to emancipate himself from the slavery of commitment to duty. Things had been blissful for a month, until he could no longer stand the voice of his conscience when he was alone. Now he was alone, thinking over the consequences of his self-determination.

"They'll raise a family to hate me" he thought, grandly. "She won't forget our time together. She will tell him stories." His mind briskly flipped through the scenes of his personal epic and culminated in the tragedy of the present.

The woman in red got a call, picked it and walked to the back of the bar. He leaned towards the vacancy she had left to catch her lingering scent.

I'm Fine

Karen Okundayor Bright-Davies

I'm awake.

I know this because I'm suddenly aware that I am in my room. I'm not sure where I was some moments ago, but it was definitely not here. My dreams tend to do that.

I wiggle my toes. They move. I am awake.

I still haven't opened my eyes. I'm thinking of going back to sleep. It's a sweet thought but I know I mustn't. I part my eyelids. For a second, I'm not sure if they really are open or closed. I blink. Yes, they are open, but it's really hard to tell because ECG has done its thing again; the entire space is pitch black. My alarm is still beeping faintly in my left ear. I reach my arm under the pillow and bring the phone to my face. God, the light is blinding! I squint and quickly tap *dismiss*. I lower the brightness on my phone to save my retinas. 5:03 am. Morning. At this realization, my heart sinks.

I'm so tired. I have to be at work in a few. The traffic is going to be bad. I'll be late. Ugh … Bad.

I'm such a bad person. I shouldn't have followed him to his room yesterday. I bet he thinks I'm a slu— …

Room. Bed. Clothes.

Dammit, I didn't iron my clothes! Now the lights are out, how will I … Lights. Phone. Text.

Ekow. He still hasn't texted after I slipped him my number. I need to get him to notice me … Notice. Ignore.

Chukwu didn't reply my WhatsApp last night. I saw the blue ticks. Is he ignoring … Ignore. Sad. Empty.

I always feel so empty. Nothing fills. Why? Maybe if I was rich … Rich. Money.

Oh God, I forgot to withdraw money from the ATM machine last night! I'll have to …

Money. Today.

Oh shoot, I still haven't written the story! Deadline today. I'm such a lazy fu— … Lazy. Relax. Mellow. High.

I haven't smoked one in a while. Lisa said she could hook me up… Hook up. Date.

I hope Kwabena isn't still mad at me. I didn't plan for the date to go sour …

Till this moment, I feel nothing. But the thoughts are soon followed by a crashing wave of random emotions drowning me. My heart beats faster. I can't breathe properly. I'm angry. I'm guilty. I'm conniving. I'm hurt. I'm lonely. I'm frustrated. I'm tired.

I'd cover my ears but this cacophony is not from outside. I'd scream to overshadow it but I'd wake the family. Underneath my cover cloth, I grab my upper arm and dig my nails deep into my flesh as I grit my teeth and squeeze my eyes shut. I feel nothing. My immunity has increased. I dig deeper till I have no more strength, till the feeling of emotional pain is exchanged with its physical counterpart. It's temporary, I know. But it will do for now. Till tomorrow morning.

I breathe in and breathe out to stabilize my heart rate. I swallow back the lump in my throat and tilt my head back so the tears don't roll down. There are footsteps approaching my door. Someone is awake. Daddy, probably. I hear a switch click right outside my room. A glow seeps in through my window. The lights are back. Almost immediately my door swings open and my father's face pokes through. He notices I am awake and smiles.

"Good morning, darling." he says cheerfully. "How are you?"

I take in a deep breath, put on my best pretend smile and reply, "I'm fine".

The Kelewele Seller

Karen Okundayor Bright-Davies

When her eyelids parted, she was immediately unsure she had really opened her eyes. Lying still, all she could see was a disturbing pitch darkness. Slowly, her tiny hands registered feeling. Then her back. Then her buttocks and legs. She felt folds of cloth beneath her, but the surface underneath the cloth was hard and rough. She was lying in a warm, funny-smelling liquid; the cloth had done a poor job of soaking it up and it was all over her legs and thighs. Confused, she sat up sharply and in panic. Her eyes tried to focus and adjust to the darkness but all she could see were oddly shaped silhouettes randomly moving about.

It wasn't too silent, there were voices. Some extremely loud, some faint, none she could recognize. They made odd sounds, nothing she could understand, and they seemed to come at her from all directions. There were footsteps pitter-pattering non-stop in odd rhythms around her. Her sharp ears picked up one particular set, its consistent pattern began faintly and seemed to get louder and louder; they were approaching steadily in her direction. She opened her mouth to scream, but there seemed to be a marble stuck in her throat. She tried to get up but her legs could not carry her. She rolled over onto her stomach, lifted herself on all fours, and began to crawl as fast as she could. In what direction, she didn't know. All she wanted to do was scramble away, fast.

Before she could get far, large coarse hands grabbed her from behind. Her eyes widened to the size of fists as she watched the ground move further and further away from her. She flailed her arms and legs wildly, thrashing as hard as she could. The scream lodged in her throat pushed its way upward, but the marble wouldn't budge. It hurt. Water filled her eyes but not a tear dropped. The blurry world began to turn slowly…no, she was the one being turned by the hands. In a split-second adrenalin hit the ceiling, the marble popped out of her throat, the tears in her eyes had reached the brim and the first of them was about to drop. Before she realized it, she was face to face with … a face.

"Ei, my child, where are you running off to?" the night kelewele seller exclaimed. She picked up her baby from under her display table. Spread upon the table were strips of cardboard boxes carrying the deliciously spicy fried plantain. Two kerosene lamps stood by. "Oh! And you have urinated on yourself too!"

Culinary Musings

Kiiki Quarm

Mama Akos huffs and puffs and grinds her onions.

"A whole Akosua Adjeiwaa! He did this to me! A whole me!"
She stops. Placing her arms akimbo, her face is a picture of
disbelief.

"Look at me from the top of my head to the bottom of my two
feet. *How?*"

Maakos throws in two blood-red tomatoes and pummels them
with her grinder.

"I am beautiful, certainly more than she is. My skin is one
colour throughout, while she has patches all over." She hits the
tomatoes. "That Vero, she thinks Carotone will save her. *Kai!*"
The abuse on the tomatoes continues, and into the *asanka* go
four *kpakpo shito*, extra-large. "If even it was a simple matter of
tasting another woman, I could understand. Men are allowed
to taste." The muscles in her forearm look like pistons as she

moves her hands back and forth in rage. "But to go after that...that rat!"

Pause.

"Ah, Sylvanus! You are a very foolish man!"

Maakos kisses her teeth, a resounding *mtcheeeeeew*, and goes back to grinding. More onions. "How can you go for Vero? Vero!" She huffs and puffs and kisses her teeth again. "That ugly

Vero whose daughter will not even speak to her because Pastor Mensah says it is she who has caused poor Rose's barrenness. It is that one that you like?"

Maakos lifts the *asanka* and pours its contents over the meaty broth steaming over her coal pot. The smell that hits her in the face is glorious to her nostrils.

"I mean, even if you are going to close a womb, at least do it well. How can you get caught? Bleaching, you can't do. Witchcraft too, you can't do."

Maakos puts her face to the pot again. As the soup bubbles, the bones bob up and down. She smiles. The juice is always in the bones.

"It is an incompetent witch that you want eh, Sylvanus?"

She fans the fire; the *papa* slaps the sides of the coal pot, its earrings dance.

"You had a whole Akosua Adjeiwaa, whose father is the don dada of this whole township, and it is ordinary Vero whose fruit you wanted to pluck! Eh, Sylvanus? *Eh*?"

Maakos rises, and it is difficult to tell which has the brighter flame; her eyes or the charcoal.

"Obaa Yaa! Yaa!"

"Yes Ma!"

"Come and watch my soup. I'm going out." "Yes Ma."

Maakos tucks her cutlass into her girdle. In one stealth movement, her cloth is wrapped around her great waist. She stomps off.

Before she exits the compound, Akosua Adjeiwaa looks back at her boiling husband in disgust.

"Don't worry, Sylvanus. Your witch is coming."

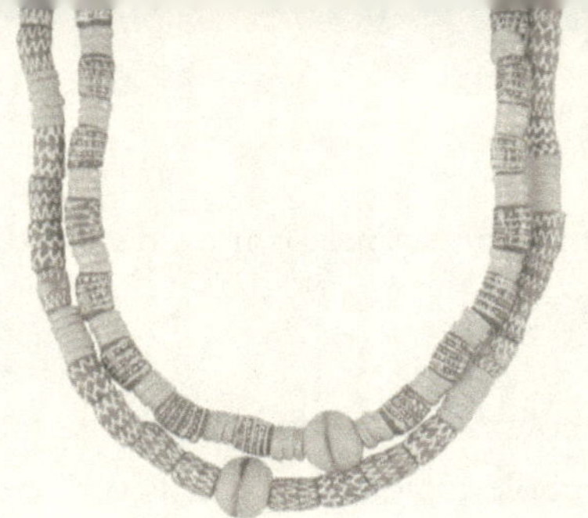

Ritual Penance

Kuukua Asante

Nii Afotey bent over the aluminium bucket with his shovel in hand. He diligently scrubbed the shovel with a metal gauze and soap. He was once a mason but that was a long time ago, when he still had youthful hair on his head and teeth that could bite bones. Now his only pastime was doing menial jobs around his compound and scrubbing his precious shovel weekly.

Mansa, Afotey's wife and her sister, Tawiah, looked on. They still could not understand Afotey's obsession with that particular shovel. It was so old and rusty; the handle was broken and one screw on the shaft was missing. Still Nii wouldn't let go of the shovel. Tawiah often teased her sister that she had a shovel for a rival, and though Mansa laughed along her sister's jokes, she occasionally caught herself giving it some thought. Today they had the same weekly conversation.

Afotey listened to the women's chatter in the porch. He knew what they were thinking, they had asked him so many times but he never said a word in response. He continued scrubbing in silence. As he scrubbed he ran his hand over a small dent in the back of the blade. That dent was part of the reason the shovel had become a sacred object to him.

Afotey's mind took him to the path that led to his farm. He had just finished work on his site and was heading home, but he decided to uproot some tubers of yam to give to Mansa his betrothed. She was a beautiful lady and of wealthy lineage, so he had to make sure her parents understood that he could take care of her. Already, Kojo from the big city had started making advances at her. Afotey could tell, from the attitude of Mansa's mother, that she preferred Kojo to him. After all, Kojo was rich, and from the same tribe.

He recalls meeting Kojo at the crossroads to his farm. No one knows about their encounter and Afotey has hidden the truth in his heart for so long he no longer remembers vividly. Now he's unsure what really took place. Only snippets remain … the sound of a gun… The instinctive shielding with the shovel… The retaliatory smacking of the assailant… Moans of pain…blood…

Kojo was buried a week after Afotey and Mansa's marriage ceremony. The couple moved to the big city soon after. He took his shovel along and though he worked as a carpenter, he never disposed of the implement. Each week, he would bring it out and scrub it thoroughly. It was a form of penance ritual for him. But no matter how long or hard he scrubbed, he still couldn't wipe those snippets of memory…especially the blood…out of his head.

Afotey rinsed the shovel and raised it against the sun. The shovel was so clean it glistened in the midday sun. Yet, he knew he would bring it out again the next week, and the week after, for his weekly penance.

Mutilated

Kwabena Agyare Yeboah

Canaan abɔnten so ɛhɔ na yɛbɛtena daada
Yɛretutu yenan
Te sɛ deɛ akwantufo tutu no

I look on at my corpse as the mourners sing this Akan dirge. In a rusty black metallic bed covered with a white wrapper I lie, dressed in the same white gown I wore on my wedding day. I wear a frozen smile that gallantly radiates under the neon light. The smile is a gift from my embalmer. Out of benevolence, he decided to make me the most beautiful corpse that he has ever worked on. He spent long hours giving me this complete make-over. He was successful. He thinks our ancestors will be glad to see me smiling. A smile is considered a gesture of acceptance; acceptance of one's fate. I should owe him gratitude. But no, I cannot be an ancestor.

They have erected a tent outside my father's house. A group of mourners sit and wait their turn to view my body. They murmur about my death. The varying reports about the state of my body continue to bewilder them. They are here to confirm the truth of what they've heard.

My body lies in my mother's room. She sits by my side and narrates folktales, just as she did three months ago during my wedding ceremony. The bed squeaks a little with each sentence. A smile blossoms on her face and then burns out like a candle's light. For the first time in weeks, Papa has left her side. He has stationed himself in front of the door leading to her room. He has appointed himself a bouncer to drive away those who cannot shut their mouths. He cannot contain himself. He sobs loudly.

My husband stands with Papa. For a grieving widower, he has stuffed himself with an incredible amount of courage. From time to time, he teaches Papa how to hold back the tears, how to be a man. I wish I could pull all three of them into an eternal family hug.

My body is a strange object now. It has been manicured to hide the mutilations. It will be a disappointment for many of the nosey mourners who have come to see me for the last time. In our tradition, bodies are intentionally mutilated for ritualistic reasons, so that they will not be accepted into the ancestral world. My mutilations are not intentional.

I was returning from a church service, slowly making my way towards my home, when I was knocked over from behind. I lay on the ground, panting for just a short time. My broken tibia could not carry me. Blood began to gush out of my slit neck. My hand grew cold as I struggled to stop the blood flow. I knew I wanted to hold on to life more than anything, but when death makes a gentle tap on your shoulder, you know it is time to sail home.

I lost consciousness and never regained it. But my killer did not leave my body untouched. He slashed my vagina with a short knife and tossed it into a bin. By the time he was done, my upper frame was tattooed with machete marks. That was how I died. As a disembodied spirit.

I am the first child of my parents to die. Many of the familial spirits are here at my funeral, unseen by human eyes. There is a grand welcome for every spirit. However, one's fate as a citizen of the land of ancestors, Npomu, has to be decided by Amɔkye, the eternal gateman.

When I died, my spirit wandered. I stayed on the shore of this mortal life and waited for Amɔkye to sail me home. I watched as he sailed others to the land of the ancestors. But he never stopped to look my way. I was another Moses who saw Canaan but never stepped foot there. I patiently waited for my turn. And then one day, he trained his eyes at me and spoke in a low voice. He said that my death was unnatural and because of that I could not be an ancestor. He sat by me and narrated the history behind my "unnatural death".

He told me I was an incarnation of my great grandmother, Yaa Akono. She had a brother. He was Kofi Agyekum, a hunter. Their family was the poorest in the land at the time. Once, Kofi returned from hunting with a new wife. He confided in Yaa, telling her about how he got into the forest and met an antelope which spoke to him and promised to make him rich if he would marry it. He agreed to the proposal and the antelope instantly morphed into the most beautiful woman in the land. They married and the entire family became rich.

But envy grew between the siblings. One day, there was a confrontation between the two. Yaa, in the heat of the moment, revealed Kofi's secret in public. Kofi's wife heard the secret revealed, and cursed my lineage with death before returning to the forest where Kofi had met her. My great grandmother, Yaa, travelled to a farther land. Ever since then, Kofi has passed on his revenge mission through different lifetimes. I was the last from Yaa's lineage and from now on, I would live eternally as a ghost.

My father will lead the procession that will bury me in the afternoon. I will retire from earthly duty. I will wander. I will live. Just like a ghost. Kwadwo Mensah, Kofi incarnate, my distant cousin, is still at large.

Blistered Memory

Kwaku Asiedu Benneh

Kwesi awoke and fixed his eyes on the T&J ceiling fan. It whirred above his head like a halo. He swivelled, then cringed, once again noting the body pains from playing soccer on Saturday evenings.

A simmering ache shot through his knee and lower back when he dared to stand. He sat still and observed. Abena would have laid the suit cover in the armchair across the room. Also in the armchair will be his white suit and black pants, starched and pressed, with a bright coloured necktie for that punch. Mother made him wear this uniform on the last Sunday of every month "so people will see you are from a good home".

He stayed longer in the shower. He stood there and let the water pierce his back like a thousand hot needles while he watched the steam rise and fill the cubicle. It was a sweet sort of pain, this home-brewed therapy.

When he was done, he smeared himself with Shea butter and lightly applied Sporting Waves to the sides of his hair. He smiled at the mirror: service will be good today.

Mama walked out in her Kente kaba and slit. She picked her Bible from the stool in the corner of the hall and planted it in her bag. She dusted her cheeks, smoothened her eyebrows and brushed past him, exuding a relaxed pretence of what her faith taught her to be. She carried an air of chatty happiness and vibrating warmth every Sunday morning, a mien she promptly cast away when the family returned from service.

Papa's Land Cruiser backed out of the garage and honked twice. The second blast was always prolonged. Somehow, it reminded Kwesi of Abena's screams the night she scalded herself with boiling water.

That night, Abena was in the kitchen, half impaired by the wan light of the only candle in the room. She turned off the burner and wrapped a thick napkin around the handles of the saucepan filled with boiling water. The steam rose to her face and she blew steadily over the pan to drive it away. Then she headed out, loudly warning about what she was transporting, "Me kita nsuo hye , me kita nsuo hye ".

She turned and nudged the kitchen door open with her back and was making her way toward Papa's half-empty bucket when the old man himself swung the door open. It slammed into her. A scream escaped the back of her throat as she tripped backwards and collapsed. The hot water was everywhere; on the floor and walls, her skirt and chest, her face. The saucepan danced and clanged until it settled. Her moaning filled the uncomfortable dark.

Mama turned into her Sunday self that night. She did not wait to apportion blame. Instead, she bundled the screaming maid into her car and drove her to the hospital. Papa remained at home, confused. The lights came back on much later and Mama returned with the girl to meet Papa still in his great white towel, seated in the living room in funereal silence. Abena had been treated and bandaged on her face, her neck and her chest. We could not stand the look of it, her swollen eyes and the smell of ointment.

Abena said she was tired of city life. She wanted to go back to the settled peace of her own home. No one objected. Mama sent her back to her village with more luggage than she came with and a lot of money. Kweku remembered her screaming voice anytime the lights went off. He worried about the memories she might have of them. Perhaps she would remember last Christmas when she got a present like she was a member of their family. Or maybe New Year's Day at Kokrobite beach. Perhaps she kept the picture Kwaku drew of her when he asked her to be his Valentine. He didn't think she even knew what he meant, but she threw her arms round him and took a bite of his chocolate.

Kwesi slid into the back of his dad's car and winced. He wondered if she still thought of his brother.

A Trotro Week

Nana Adwoa Amponsah-Mensah

Yaw Akyea stood still with his left hand holding on to the railing above him to keep steady. She was pressed so closely to him he could feel her lacy top through his coat. Two other women stood on either side of him with their backs turned. There was little wiggle room so various body parts kept rubbing against each other. This would've been a great scene to the beginning of a fantasy if it wasn't instead on a crammed rush hour train into the city.

He stood still, trying not to move. He didn't want to make lacy-bra-woman feel self- conscious, he guessed she had plans that night. He snickered to himself and drew looks from the other unsmiling faces on the 8:20 South-Eastern service to Charring Cross. He shook his head as he cast his mind back to when he worked in the Silver Star Towers in Accra.

He used to drive his Skoda Fabia to work in town. It seemed that no matter what time he woke up, two hundred other people set their alarm clocks for the same time. Mornings were spent crawling through the traffic jam between Haatso and 37. The sun would start out smiling softly, deceitful. As soon as you rolled down your window, it would turn up the heat full blast and startle you back into your air-conditioned interior. Yaw tried to avoid looking at the fast-falling fuel gauge on some of those mornings. He'd readjust his tie as he listened to the Super Morning Show on Joy Fm. Kojo Yankson and his guests only really held his attention for so long before he'd switch to the BBC Africa channel; he preferred his bad news in a clipped British accent.

There was that one week his car spent at the mechanic when he had to make the Haatso-37 journey by trotro. That journey was as cramped and as stuffy as his present one; it was less lacy-top and starchier suit though. When he got on the trotro at his junction, he had to scurry in quickly to avoid the door slamming into him as the driver hurried to slip into the line of winding traffic at the mate's shout of, "Away!"

Yaw sat down heavily in the back seat near the window, next to a dozing man. He was snoring lightly; it made Yaw wonder what kind of night he'd had to make him fall asleep on this trotro. "Hey, take your *bati* eyes off me!" Somehow, he'd woken up and caught Yaw staring at him. The dozing man glared at him as he wiped drool off with the back of his right hand. The other passengers turned to glance at the man in the navy-blue suit and matching tie, and his accuser who wore a white shirt and burgundy tie. Their looks were part amusement and part disdain. Yaw quickly turned to look outside the window. *Great, now I won't only be late to work but about 10 Ghanaians think I'm gay.* He looked up to the greying sky, *I love Mondays,* he thought wryly.

"We will be arriving shortly at Waterloo East, please check that you take all your personal belongings when leaving this train…" The disembodied automatic voice brought him back to his spot as the ham in the woman-burger. He inched slightly to the left to allow lacy-top to reach the door of the train. The area at his back where she'd been pressed against him felt warm as he stepped off behind her. He stepped off and collided into her back; she'd stopped to wear her coat. "I'm so sorry!" she said hurriedly. Yaw noted that her accent sounded like home. He smiled at her, "Don't worry about it, have a nice day." He hurried off towards the exit, remembering a similar encounter he had had, that trotro week in Accra.

By Wednesday, he was better at getting onto the trotro. He managed to sit down before the mate yelled "away!" There was a drizzle that morning but there wasn't as much traffic, and he was sure he wouldn't be late.

At the *Spanner* traffic lights, resilient hawkers were toting items and holding them up to car windows. A young girl carried sliced pawpaws in a tray balanced on her head. She was weaving between the stationary cars when she bumped into the windshield wiper seller. Her tray went flying. Two motorbikes zipped past and crushed her pawpaws. She stood there, confused. The other hawkers were yelling at the disappearing riders; she just stood there. Yaw felt a kinship with her; her lost look was like his had been, on the trotro that Monday. "Pssst, madam!" he called out to her. She walked to him with a question in her eyes. Yaw handed her a Ten cedi note, "Have a nice day". The lights turned green. As his trotro took off, she grabbed the note and yelled, "Medaase!" Unlike the Southeastern, however, the stares he got from the other commuters were accompanied with verbal reactions, some muttered, some aloud. "You have money to waste eh?" "Ei akoa wei paa" "Oh but that was very kind oh". Yaw ignored them, he was having a good week.

At Opeibea, as he made to get off, a man trying to get on at the same time bumped into him. He instinctively held his bag closer to his body and stepped back to allow the man to squeeze in past him. The trotro chugged away leaving smoke in its wake as Yaw looked left, right and started to cross the road to the Silver Tower. He reached into his pocket to call his mechanic. When his hand came up empty, he stopped in his tracks in the middle of the road, he immediately knew that man on the trotro had his iPhone 5. "Bloody hell!"

If Undelivered

Nana Adwoa Amponsah-Mensah

Dear Ma,

I was sitting here thinking to myself how I miss the Indian almond tree that grew at the back of our house. I miss the colours of the leaves in dry season, and how they would crush under our feet, when we played in piles of leaves. I miss picking up ripe almond fruit that had fallen down and eating them without washing. I know you didn't approve; I'm sorry. I miss cracking the almond with a rock after eating the pulp, as we tried to reach the nut inside it. Those were fun times. Ma, I miss you.

I remember the day we saw a snake under the hedges next to the almond tree and you wouldn't let me or Paa go out by ourselves. We were so upset. We thought you were being wicked. I wish you had explained to us that you were protecting us the only way you knew how. Maybe if you had explained, we would've understood.

You wouldn't let us out of the house after school. Poor Paa couldn't go out to talk to his crush, Esi, for a week. You knew she wasn't in our school and he only got to see her after school. He was angry for days; I was angry for him too. Ma, maybe if you'd explained the nuances of a mother's love and the need to coddle the ones you bore, we would've understood. I'm going through the same thing now and I find that I can't properly explain it to Ekua. I think she hates me now. But all I'm doing is trying to love her!

She came home the other day in all of her 16-year-old pomp and drama, announcing that she had a boyfriend. I was more thrilled than upset. I never told you about Eli, or Kuku, so I was happy she was telling me. She gushed about Kwabena Nti endlessly. I was happy to listen; it was a nice break from my day of cleaning and cooking. I sat with her at the kitchen table and we talked till Kwesi came in from work. Even he looked surprised to see us huddled over the table giggling.

Ma, it was one of the best days of my motherhood. I understand now how you felt when I spent time telling Auntie Ewuresi and not you, about my crushes. Kwesi laughed at me later that night when I shared how happy I was that Ekua had confided in me, "Let's not get too excited oh," he had warned lightly.

Naturally, I wanted to meet the boy. When I dropped her off at her boarding house that term, I waited for her to get him from the boys' house. Ma, imagine my shock when my little Ekua emerged with a television pole of a man professing to be eighteen years old. The boy's facial hair would've made Kwesi jealous.

"Good morning, Auntie."

"Good morning Kwabena, how are you?" "I'm fine, thank you. You look lovely".

I was taken aback by his deep voice and his forward way with me. I liked his confidence; but I immediately started to worry. I wasn't sure I wanted to leave my daughter with this confident man-boy for a whole term. Before I left, I pulled her aside and tried to put on my best, breezy, 'un-motherly' tone.

"Ekua, I like him, he seems nice."

"Oh yay! Thank you, Mama! I'm so glad you do!" She squealed. When I only blinked, she cocked her head to one side.
"But?" she asked; my smart Ekua. I laughed.
"But be careful. Call me if you need to talk, okay?"

"Mama, if that's your way of asking me not to sleep with him, you've got it", she mock saluted and gave me a hug before running to take Kwabena's hand. He waved as well and made off with my baby.

Ma, I was relieved when she and I had had 'the talk'. I know ours didn't go so well. Remember how you handed me off to Da when I got my first menstrual period? He didn't know what to say, so Paa ended up stealing a book, "The Complete Tween", from the school library, for me to read instead. But Ma, I think your non-talk with me went better than my pseudo talk with Ekua.

We are seated in a sterile waiting room at a building in Korle Gonno. It looks like a normal house, white and ordinary, but inside, it is where girls come to get rid of the evidence of their lost innocence. If you listen quietly, I swear you will hear the muffled cries of foetuses wailing as they are scraped out and denied a chance to live.

That man-boy got Ekua pregnant, Ma! I was so furious when she told me. I dragged her here after my friend told me about this place. Nurse Jackson from church said that these days all regular hospitals do it. She advised that we go to one at Airport. Ma, how can I take my baby to a regular hospital to get mutilated like it's normal? I prefer this back-alley way, it looks as shady as it feels. I think it's only right.

Ekua has cried for a week since I told her we were doing this. She hasn't spoken to or even looked me or Kwesi in the eye for days. Ma, I'm afraid she hates me. Why? I never once blamed you for the time you and I sat in this same position. I knew it was my fault and I had to do it.

Ma, I'm sitting here thinking about Indian almonds, my childhood, and my baby's baby, because I miss you. You were always much stronger than I am. I wish you were here to hold her hand the way you held mine.

I wish you would get this letter once I finish it. I wish you were alive.

Love,
Akosua Akyaa.

Mr. Almost-Perfect

Nana Adwoa Amponsah-Mensah

She had that familiar feeling in her chest; the burning sensation she got when she was really angry or ate too much gari. Her vision blurring with tears, she placed her phone on her bed and started putting on her clothes with a strange calmness. Following the trail of clothes on the floor of her bedroom, she caught herself thinking it was like a Christian Grey version of Hansel and Gretel. She stepped over his white shirt and reached for her jeans.

"Sneaking out, are we? Aren't I supposed to do that?" He jested from the doorway of the bathroom. She kept her back to him, and finished dressing up. "Adobea?"

Stepping into her shoes, she turned and picked up her phone. "Adobea? Everything okay?" He closed the gap between them and tried to hold her.

She held her hands in front of her, she wasn't ready to use any words because she was afraid she would break down and cry.

Adobea took his hand off her arm and held out her hands again.

"Please leave"

She turned around and walked out. Wiping her tears and blowing loudly into a piece of tissue she had randomly picked up.

She looked at her phone, read the last message for the tenth time and texted:

"How do you know?"

"Facebook stalking. I'm sorry" came the instant reply.

Adobea was picking up lunch from the cafeteria on a busy day. On days like this, she preferred the solitude of her desk to the loud cafeteria atmosphere.

She looked up from her phone to see him asking whether the seat opposite her was available. She grunted a response as he sat down and she went back to checking her Instagram feed. Adobea looked up again, this time, to catch him glancing at her chest. She wore a white buttoned-up shirt but that never made a difference. People stared anyway, mostly because they found her too small to own a bust this size. She smirked and liked one more picture.

"Do you work in this building?" he asked.

"Yes, do you?"

"No, just visiting a friend. He's stuck in a meeting so I thought I'd grab lunch first." *"Okay"*, she muttered.
"So, what do you do?"

Adobea sighed. She could already imagine him asking for her number and texting her to go out on a date. She usually tried to be nice about the random pick-ups, but it'd been a long day at the Fast Track court; it seemed all her seniors at the Bar had motions to move that morning. She'd spent four hours at the court earlier and now, all she wanted was fried yam with some fish.

"I'm a lawyer" she responded, mentally making a note to scream if he said "I put it to you", "my learned friend" or any of the other clichés she had grown to hate.

"I'm a fan of lawyers" he said beaming a smile her way. She raised her eyebrows and smiled, in spite of herself.

"And what do you do?" *"I'm a writer"*
"Well, I happen to be a fan of writers."

One of the servers brought Adobea her pack; it seemed unusually quick. They had barely spoken for a couple of minutes and she found herself hoping he'd ask for her number.

She reached into her purse and handed him a business card, "In case you ever need a lawyer."

He laughed and read it aloud "Adobea D. Bram," turning to her he extended his hand, "it was nice meeting you, Adobea.

She was waiting for the elevator when her phone vibrated:

"In case you ever need a writer, Miss Bram."

Their first date was after a month of cryptic texts and subtle flirting. He'd texted her that Saturday morning,

"Hey, I'm stepping out for a bit. Can I see you?" Adobea liked how easy he was; it made whatever they had seem effortless.

"Sure. When?"

"After 7pm. Wait for my call, please"

"Ha! Should I sit by my phone and bite my nails as well? Aye-aye Captain!"

Adobea was sitting in the dryer at the salon with her friend Efua when the text startled her. She had brought Efua along for moral support and also to bring her up to speed on her newly rekindled fandom of writers. It was still an hour to "after 7pm".

"Hey. Too early?" "Depends"
"On what, babe?"

"On where you intended to meet me at" "I'll come wherever you are…"
"Then no, not too early."

"Sister Awo, mepaakyɛw awo wai" Adobea all but barked at the hairdresser. She didn't care that her curls would possibly go limp overnight.

"Oh, daabi, aka kakra", the hairdresser insisted. Adobea stood up and started to pull out the curlers. The disgruntled woman took over and combed through the partially curled hair, scowling.

They met in the car park of the Highgate Hotel. He parked his car and slid into the passenger seat of hers bearing gifts; chocolate-glazed doughnuts and Kelewele. They ended up talking and listening to the radio in the car park for over two hours. Adobea felt a closeness and easiness about their conversation that she hadn't felt in a long time.

Eventually, they drove to her apartment. As they climbed upstairs hand-in-hand, he pulled her close and said in an almost whisper,

"I wish you were mine"

"Aren't I?"

She circled her arms around his neck and they kissed slowly. As he reached to unbutton her shirt, she felt her phone vibrate. It could only be Efua checking on how her date had gone.

That could wait.

Adobea woke when he got up to use the bathroom later that night. She checked her phone. Efua hadn't been checking how the date went,

"Bea, do you know he is married?"

The Flood

Nii Moi Thompson

The fiery flame was vaporizing my wax; I was growing shorter by the minute. Cached in one corner on a Milo tin on top of an old wall between mould-smeared walls and furniture, under rotting window frames, silhouetted against peeling paint flaunting damp patches, my drooling wax was the least of my concerns. It was the rain. It was battering the leaking aluminium roofing sheets in heavy torrents. As Sima lifted her baby from the plastic bathing basin, she realised I was almost dead.

"I need to replace this candle, but your drunken father is now sprawled in his own vomit at the liquor shop, I know. Who will go out to get candles now?" I could hear her grumbling to herself.

Just then, I heard paws pounding on the door amidst incessant whining as though the pounder was being pursued. And as Sima stretched to turn the knob while clutching her baby, the family dog rushed in, furiously shaking off droplets of rainwater from its fur.

"The rain might get worse. I have to go buy some candles quickly," Sima finally resolved.

She left me and the dog in charge of the baby, who was lying on the mattress in peaceful slumber with the basin at the bed's foot, unperturbed by the heavy downpour. I continued to light their darkness, yet not for long…

My cloud-sons are locking airs again, thundering and spitting rapid fire at one another. They were condensed hence had to splash their fury on earth. So, they splashed, softly and rationally at first, until even I, the Sky god, could neither rest nor control them. I noticed as Sima, coated in hand-made polythene robe waded through the sparse puddles of water to get candles ahead of what might be a long, dark night.

I quivered at the consequence of what mere mortals would have to bear as a result of defiling the earth goddess, and spitting fume in my own face. Man has pushed me to my extremes. When I rain, I pour. When I burn, I scorch. I quivered for Sima and the little mortal she had abandoned in the darkness. She splashed and stumbled out of the marsh in which their house was seated; past the gutter by which her husband had built their house; up the dumpsite along the snaky pathway with scattered household units arranged in no coherent pattern. I heard her thoughts: "If these trees hadn't been cut, people would not have built their houses in the water's way".

The trees had been sawed into strong planks to construct a small bridge across a deep gorge created by the furious splashes of my cloud-sons. Sima trod cautiously over the bridge.

My cloud-sons splashed more rapidly…

"Can I get two candlesticks, please," Sima requested, wholly drenched by the rain.

"Ei Aunty Sima, you hardly visit us these days," the little attendant sparked off some conversation as she hopped onto a stool in order to reach the shelf.

"Was Oko Papa here today?" Sima moved on to weightier matters. Oko Papa was her husband. Everybody called him that.

"Yes oo. He took two shots of the regular, danced around for a while and headed home when the sky threatened grey". Though she hated the attendant's garrulous tongue, Sima seemed apathetic. She had grown immune to Oko Papa's buffoonery.

Before she could pay for the candlesticks, the attendant pointed her finger precipitously with shock on her face.

"Look, Aunty Sima," she screamed, "The bridge is being washed away."

Initially, I felt the severity of the situation did not dawn on Sima judging by her lax approach to the news, until she opened her eyes in horror and exclaimed, "My baby".

I observed from my Sky throne—hands tied—a poor mother dashing through the rain in utmost despair and fright for her lonely baby about to drown. And true, the gorge was her dead end. For when she got to it she noticed the rain had swept the wooden bridge away, filling the gorge to its brim and copiously cascading down the dumpsite towards their home with such rough force. She started yelling for help, but the rain drowned her voice…

The situation was getting dire. I had almost burnt my wick to my own death, save several inches sitting in the liquid of my wax. Yet I gave the baby a faint glow of hope. The rain was crawling in from underneath the door. It had filled the room, swallowing the legs of the bed, with the plastic basin floating tumultuously atop. The dog was barking and howling, loud enough to awaken the sleeping baby who started a little supplication for relief on its own, shrieking and kicking.

I was thankful when the door squeaked open.

Oko Papa staggered into the room, his eyes bloodshot, wielding a liquor bottle, sensing danger yet too drunk to react swiftly. He fell heavily in the pool, and dragged himself through it to reach his blood.

The door was ajar. The water flooded the room rapidly. The rain crept up the wall unit and swept away the Milo tin on which I stood. I fell, a splash…BLACKOUT!

Sima was still waiting by the gorge when her neighbours arrived with her baby, clad in warm clothes, safe and cackling.

"We found her floating in the basin".

Sima held her baby guardedly, as she would a missing but found nugget.

"He drowned while trying to save your baby, we presume", one man told Sima as Oko Papa's body was ferried by on a board by do-gooders, all wrapped in a traditional funeral cloth.

The Well

Nii Moi Thompson

"Ao! Here, suck my breast!" Maku made one last futile attempt to guide her nipple into her baby's mouth, but he would just nibble on it briefly with his milk teeth, and then resume the ear-deafening bawling over nothing, at the highest octave possible.

The old man observed intently. "Strap the baby up," he resolved. "I think what it needs is a good nap." She obeyed, as her husband, Kweikuma, paced their tiny living room, taking giant strides—heaving angry sighs.

"Numo'e, this woman has no shame." Kweikuma knitted eyebrows and gritted yellow teeth. He was a carpenter—nailing and sawing planks for a living. His friends and the mirror often told him his head was of no regular shape, and that his dental formula was incalculable. He possessed a plain face, however, paradoxically coupled with an impatient and haughty personality.

"Calm your nerves, young man," Numo'e cautioned. "Hot temper is like a fierce forest fire. It destroys not only the woods, but also the game therein."

"Anyway, old man," Kweikuma snapped. "Maku, this woman here is an adulteress. I don't want her as a wife anymore. Agbenaa!"

The old man's eyes swept the narrow living room. It was quite well-furnished. Its soft, comfy sofa with handsome embroidery rested in a carapace of an Ivorian mahogany frame; legs tipped in golden stands. The ceiling fan was the latest Binatone, and the floor was turfed with a red carpet flaunting beautiful zig-zag patterns. The light-blue bulb illuminated the room, painting their silhouettes against the impeccable wall where their engagement picture hung uncertainly.

On the centre-table were 6 pieces of GTP clothes, a box of jewellery, a ring, six pieces of headscarf, a Methodist hymn book, a Bible, Bottles of Gin and Whisky, some crates of assorted soft drinks and a 1986 Butterfly sewing machine. There was a bold inscription engraved on the sewing machine, reading: PROVERBS 5:15-20. "…And these items?" Numo'e queried.

Kweikuma shrugged, "Well, I'm returning her to her people. I cannot live with a promiscuous wife. Everybody eats from her bowl."

Numo'e chuckled and glanced at Maku, who had cupped her chin in her right hand, shaking her head disbelievingly while her baby napped, strapped to her back.

"Tell me," the old man probed further. "Who has eaten from her bowl?"

Kweikuma hesitated but summoned courage momentarily. He burst out, "She has been sleeping with Osabu the track driver, our neighbour who lives six houses down this street."

"Oh, Kweikuma, that's a lie. Since you stopped handing me some transport money, Osabu has been helping me by packing my vegetables into his trailer, and then dropping me off at the market every morning. That's all oo!" Maku explained, rubbing her palms in innocence, looking up to the heavens with pure, crystal eyes. "God, bear me witness."

"Shut up, Ashawo!"

"Silence!" the old man intervened. "Did you catch them sleeping together?"

Kweikuma assumed a sheepish demeanour. "Ah, b-b-but need I? Maku, if you don't confess eh…" he dashed towards Maku, fists clenched.

"To scare a bird is not the best way to catch it, Kweikuma." Numo'e advised. "Now rest your bottom."

Kweikuma did so after seconds of hesitation.

Numo'e cleared his throat. "I know your beginning very well, Kweikuma. Even during your years of practice as an apprentice. You had one white shirt turned brown, and often wore an oversized pair of trousers, which you held in check with tattered braces." Kweikuma nodded in humiliation…and discomfort.

"When you met Maku…" the old man continued. "…her vegetable business was doing well. She took care of you, fed you twice in a day, morning and evening…"

"But I was not starving to death. I had had enough of gari. I just needed some small soup to go with it." Kweikuma murmured.

Numo'e cut in. "My father often passed this axiom, that when poverty comes in at the door, love flies through the window. But Maku proved that my father did not know it all. Maku could have had any man she desired." And indeed, it was true. Maku was a thing of beauty even after one gruelling childbirth. She had features of a traditional high-life guitar, and her face had no flaws.

"Yet, I honestly do not understand why she chose to marry you. When I led you to her parents, you had just Proverbs 5:15-20 as her dowry."

Kweikuma glared at Proverbs 5:15-20, the Butterfly sewing machine he had paid as Maku's dowry.

"She shared your shack—that carpenter's shop with just a window…and I remember its roof leaked badly whenever it rained. She bore you a son…in the dangerous face of your collapsed business. However, two years ago, since you won that Chinese furniture contract, your colours changed. It is easy to glance covetously at the water in another man's well. But it is wiser to cling to the well that quenched your thirst when you were thirsty. Remember, money is a visitor—he chooses to stay depending on how well you treat him. When the mouth swallows a knife, the anus must worry about how to expel it. My son, drink from your own well!"

The old man's words sunk in deep. That night, Kweikuma, the carpenter, made love to Maku blithely on the sofa, near Proverbs 5:15-20, the memorable Butterfly sewing machine. He drank from his own well, deep and long, forgetting all about Adjoa Pee, the voluptuous, and distracting next door neighbour who had nearly marred their marriage, much to the ignorance of his dear wife and Numo'e, or so he thought.

It was February 14 when the clock struck midnight.

The Wily Twig-Men of Asempa

Nii Moi Thompson

Nobody in Asempa knew that the twig-men came to life under the moonlight to dance kete with the birds. Although the merry clinking of the gong amidst heavy kete drumbeat could be heard a few miles from Ntow's vegetable field, no one dared to sneak into the grove at such an hour, not even the bravest of hunters, lest the spirits clipped their tongues and rendered them mute.

Asem's exploited glands had no saliva left to quench the scorching of his throat, and his kennel was yet several miles away from the grove. He waddled through the dew-soaked shrubs, feeling his way with sore paws and guiding himself with light from the silvery full moon, until he realized he was at the foot of that short, thick plank which bridged his master's vegetable field and Adoma, the cashew grower's. He had been running in circles.

He cried out for help, but all any man could hear was the echoing howl of a famished predator racing across his master's farm. His paw nearly crushed a tomato.

"Now kill me before those twig-men and cruel birds do!" the tomato squelched in agony.

Asem growled and wagged his tail. A tomato cannot speak, he thought. But he was sure he heard a distinct voice.

"Who are you?" he barked.

"Quiet!" the tomato cried. It was red and juicy and ready for harvest. "The twig-men shall soon come to life, and the birds shall glide hither."

Asem burst into peals of laughter. "Don't be stupid. Those are scarecrows my master crafted with dry twigs and fastened together with thick ropes. They certainly have no life."

"Believe me," the tomato said, mirroring the moon on its shiny flesh. "Ask me why some of my friends were half -eaten a fortnight ago when you came to harvest garden-eggs with your master."

"Rodents, probably!"

"Wrong, my friend. The twig-men let the birds eat us."

Asem could feel his throbbing heart against his fur, threatening to spurt. He had little choice but to believe an outlandish tale from a talking tomato. He stared at the twig-men planted sparsely over the field. They looked still…lifeless.

"At the sound of the owl, you must hide under the little barn over there," the tomato advised. Asem knew where the barn was and inched closer. He quivered, and watched, and waited.

Ntow had gone to inspect his traps earlier that morning with his musket slung over his shoulder with Asem obediently trailing behind. The traps had caught nothing, making Asem feel sorry for his master. In sympathetic defiance, he had set off after some slippery grass- cutters, plunging deeper into the grove until he could neither find Ntow nor his way back home.

When the night got colder and the willows whistled harder, Asem's eyes shut deep in slumber right under that little barn he had taken refuge. Then, the hooting of the owl was heard and a flock of crows and fruit-eating bats descended like an army invading a small town. The twig- men were outnumbered, or so one would think.

By this time, the incessant wing-flapping and cawing and hooting had woken Asem from his sleep, and he was certain he was not dreaming.

"Sound the gong and start the *kete*," the owl hooted. "The twig-men need to move their twigs to the sacred dance."

The music came in soft at first, until it got louder, then Asem's canines rattled in his muzzle at what he saw. The twig-men came to life; the hats on their stuffed sock-heads suddenly swaying this way and that, and their eyes reddening. Their twigs moved harmoniously to the rhythm of the *kete* music, whiles the birds feasted, plunging their beaks into the ripen fruits, picking the vegetables violently. It was as though the twig-men were entertaining the birds while they ate the produce of an honest man's labour. The moonlight blessed them with a good shine; such a cruel conspiracy.

After the birds had wreaked sufficient havoc, and the twig-men had danced enough, the former flew away, flapping their victorious wings in a choreographed manner, while the latter assumed their lifeless positions on the field, with half-eaten fruits and vegetables.

Asem's bones rattled in the dark until the first golden ray pierced the dawn and broke it. He wanted to rush home to tell his master the strange tale of the birds and the twig-men, but his limbs were too weak from shock.

When his master finally arrived on the field to lament his loss, Asem tried to recount the horrid episode to him, and how the scarecrows he made had become allies to preying birds. Yet, all Ntow could hear were the exasperating barks of a found dog that got lost in the woods.

The next day Ntow made some more twig-men. Perhaps three were just not enough to scare fruit-eating bats, cawing crows and hooting owls.

Clarity

Priscilla Adipa

It happened unexpectedly. Eventually. Unlike his commitment to Augusta, the discovery took time. When he uncovered the reasons behind her phone calls and averted eyes, he saw that this point would have been reached sooner, if only he had not been overly confident in his ability to hold Augusta's attention.

He stood in the rain, his temper rising as the raindrops on top of his head grew heavier and heavier. He opened his mouth and received the rain. The weight and saltiness of the water in his mouth brought on memories of tongues locked in passion, bodies pliant to the desires of each other. Hungry for more, he pushed out his whole tongue and held it still in space. When recalling became painful, he pulled his tongue back into his mouth.

Augusta returned home to find Kwasi's drenched form stretched out on their doorstep. As soon as she saw him, she knew their journey together was over. She hesitated in the car.

Somewhere deep inside her, a breath of relief and regret came alive. Being in harmony with Kwasi had become tedious, so tedious that she had looked elsewhere for what he no longer provided. Yet, Augusta wavered. She had to be sure she was ready to let go.

Slowly, she turned off the engine. She opened the door and placed one foot onto the wet ground, and then the other. It had stopped raining. She walked towards Kwasi, her face filled with sorrow. She tried to read his thoughts, but this time, it was impossible. The force that had connected them was broken, and his mind was shut from her probing eyes.

"Kwasi." His name escaped quickly from her lips. She was breathless, as though she had run a marathon and was struggling to get her words out. "Kwasi," she called again.

He said nothing. On his face was etched a hardness Augusta had never seen before.

"Say something." She searched for absolution, a sign that all would be well between them.

In response, there was only the heavy sound of breathing and the cricket song that filled the air when the rain clouds receded.

He decided to help her out. "As long as you are happy," he said, almost too softly for Augusta to hear.

She waited for him to say more. But these were the only words that revolved around them in the growing darkness.

They stood on the doorstep, framed by the arches of the veranda. They had stood there countless times on days they escaped when it was too hot inside their small house. The doorstep was Augusta's favourite spot. It was there they sat on Fridays after work to eat *kelewele* bought from the woman down the road. It was there they spent evenings with no power, and, with just a candle and a mosquito coil between them, cursed ECG and anyone else responsible for the unending *dumsor.*

Augusta walked past Kwasi towards their front door. He had anticipated what she would need. Four suitcases stood near the door. One of the suitcases was made from a synthetic beige material with red stripes. It had remained pristine over the years. It was the suitcase Kwasi's family brought to her parents' house the morning of their engagement. It was the one they had packed with Kente and cloth she hadn't yet taken to her seamstress. All these years she'd kept the suitcase covered with a large see-through plastic bag. Now, she had to drag the suitcase on the muddied cemented ground to her car.

Again, Kwasi thought ahead of her. He grabbed hold of the bags and packed them into the car.

"Goodbye," he said, as he slammed the boot shut and made to walk back towards the house.

"I'm sorry," she said, as she placed a hand on his arm. Then, encouraged by the softening in his eyes, she leaned over to trace the angry lines on his forehead. He flinched when her hand touched his face.

"Just leave," he said, and Augusta quickly got into the car, realizing his patience would not last.

She pushed the gear into reverse when he entered the house. Her left leg shook as she lifted it off the clutch. She had all her belongings, but still it felt like she was leaving a part of herself behind. The car stalled. She put the gear again into reverse, and pulled out of their yard. She did not stop even when she looked back and thought she saw Kwasi step out onto the doorstep.

The Gush

Shefi Nelson

She felt it again and sat upright.

It was a quarter to 5am. Her neighbours were already up. She could hear Auntie Ayesua screaming for her children. The whole neighbourhood knew their names; all five. They were always late getting ready for school. Auntie Ayesua would park her silver *Citi* outside their gate and scream their names till they were seated.

Kwansima managed to smile as she recalled the first time she had met them. Ekua, the eldest, was an extremely shy girl. Kwansima could still see her struggling to balance glasses on a tray the day she and Kwesi went over. As for Kofi, the second eldest, he was known to bravely climb over the wall every time his little brother Yaw, kicked a football into Kwesi's well-groomed lawn. The twins were the most troublesome of all; Kwadwo and Adwoa took turns making sure everything in the house was broken. One minute, their father, Uncle Fiifi, was scolding the children, and then the next, Auntie Ayesua was comforting them.

She couldn't imagine having to deal with five children. Even with their first child soon to arrive, their lives had been reordered. The realities of pregnancy regularly caught them by surprise as their responsibilities escalated over the nine months.

Kwansima had always loved her three cups of coffee per-day, as she high-heeled her way through the working week. She recalled her dismay when the news broke, and she was forced to give up the ritual. She didn't even want to think about her weight gain and cravings.

Kwesi had taken a while to adjust to Kwansima's hormonal invasion. They had laughed and teased each other for years. He was dumbfounded when his harmless remark about his wife's weight had her in tears. This was during Kwansima's eighth month of pregnancy. She had cried continuously for almost an hour before they had both left home that morning. To his surprise, he returned that day to find her laughing hysterically at a movie she was watching. She knew she was supposed to be angry with him but she couldn't remember why.

There was no way she could go through this five times. No way. She laughed as she tried to imagine Kwesi's handsome face in a frown trying to grab his medical equipment from five excited children. *Her dearest* Kwesi. He had always made her proud.

The clock struck six and her thoughts went to her husband packing his black leather bag and locking up his office. He would go around to check on patients before walking the stairs two steps at a time to the car park. He would open the door diagonal to the driver's side, place his bag on the floor, shut the door, and then settle in the driver's seat for a moment. After the reassuring click of his seatbelt, he would start the engine, pleased as his beloved automobile jerked to life. He never broke the routine.

Kwansima had just started to rest her back on the bedpost when she felt it. She grabbed the bed sheets and pulled. She tried fighting it. Cautiously, she made her way to the living room, turned on the fan and settled in the couch. She idly stared at the dusty blades and thought of cleaning the house.

And cooking. It was Thursday. Kwesi loved his Banku and Tilapia on Thursdays. He always reminded her to make the banku balls soft enough to stick onto his fingers. Kwansima remembered how Kwesi hated blended pepper. She smiled, recalling the first time. He had a disturbed look on his face as he stirred the bowl with the blended pepper, looking for pieces of pepper, onions and tomatoes. In the end, she managed to turn it into sauce after cooking it with spices and large cuts of onions, tomatoes and garlic. Since then, the blender had been used for nothing but tomatoes for stew and fruits for smoothies.

The spasms interrupted her. This time, they followed one another immediately. She stared at the pictures on the walls. She tried to relax. Kwesi would soon be home. For several minutes, she struggled to regulate her breathing.

There was a faint pop, like someone had cracked a knuckle, then wetness. It didn't hurt; it was just very wet. Kwesi opened the door, Kwansima sighed.

Abena Karikari

Abena has been writing since she was eight years old. She currently works at the Institute of African Studies, University of Ghana. She lives in Accra with her husband and daughter.

Adelaide Awo Darkoa Asiedu

Adelaide is a final-year student at the University of Ghana. She has loved to read from as far back as she can remember and hopes to keep writing for as long as she can.

Akua Serwaa Amankwah

Akua Serwaa is a writer and a blogger. She's loved making stories out of words since she was eight. She's currently working on two short story collections.

Ama Asantewa Diaka

Ama Asantewa is a writer and poet based in Accra. Her work, both as a performer and a writer, engages issues of becoming, feminism, inequality, womanhood and mental health in her community. She has participated in internationally acclaimed workshops organized by Femrite (2013) and Farafina Trust (2016) and was the first poet to be selected as a OneBeat 2016 fellow.

Amanda Olive Amoah

Amanda Olive is a recent graduate of Ashesi University. She aspires to contribute to creating a world where the African child is not characterized as disadvantaged. Her favourite pastime is to get lost in daydreams.

Amma Konadu Anarfi

Amma Konadu is a reader, writer, blogger, and literary enthusiast. She loves to dabble in gourmet delights, and her other life is lived as an academic.

Anakwa Dwamena

Anakwa is a Ghanaian journalist based in Brooklyn, New York. His writing is obsessed with examining how art has flourished as a medium of protest in Ghana, and how it continues to colour and craft what we think of as our collective culture.

Ato Kwamena Bentsil

Ato Kwamena is a Business Development professional who loves mythology and fantasy tales.

Daniel Hanson Dzah

Daniel is an alumnus of the University of Ghana, Legon, where he studied Philosophy.

Edem Dotse

Edem is a writer and filmmaker living in Accra, Ghana. He is a product of Ghanaian folklore, prosperity gospel, imported television shows, hip-life music and the Internet. He seeks to explore, document and re-imagine contemporary African culture with his writing.

Ewurama Amoonua Adenu-Mensah

Ewurama is a Chemical Engineering major at Drexel University. She enjoys writing and reading historical fiction and poetry on Africa and African cultures.

Fui Can-Tamakloe

Fui spent his childhood reading everything he could. He now spends his adulthood writing short stories that showcase the world through his torchlight-underneath-covers-slightly-damaged-eyes.

Gabriella R. Rockson

Gabriella Rockson studies Dentistry but loves reading and listening to music in her spare time. When writing, she usually starts with an emotion and the rest of the story follows.

Gabriel Myers Hansen

Gabriel is a writer/pop critic with ENEWSGH and Music in Africa.

Hakeem Adam

Hakeem is an instinctive creative in love with beautiful sentences and the angst of communicating complex ideas in poetry. He frequently engages this angst with whatever creative outlet suits him best.

Ivana Akotowaa Ofori

Ivana Akotowaa is a writer and spoken word artist, but most importantly, a "lexivist" - a self- coined word that means lexical activist, one who believes in the power of words and advocates for the pursuit of word-related activities. She writes to reform, express or amuse and sometimes to do all three at once. Becoming a successful novelist is her primary aspiration in life.

Jermaine Kudiabor

Jermaine is an engineer based in Nkwatia. He writes short fiction and poetry. He's a fan of traditional Japanese forms.

Jesse Jojo Johnson

Jesse is a software developer in Accra. He writes short fiction, short essays and poetry. He does a bit of photography and music too.

Karen Okundayor Bright-Davies

Karen is a writer who tends to see intricacy in the uneventful moments of life, that makes her stop, stare and ponder. She likes to take these whiffs of life and re-present them to her readers in more detail and with a spin, so that they can see them in a way they initially could not and appreciate the beauty in all things simple.

Kiiki Quarm

Kiiki Quarm knows nothing. She is only an 18-year old who runs from anxiety by recoiling into words.

Kuukua Asante

Kuukua is a Public Relations Practitioner with a current focus on Social Media Communications in Ghana. As a regular user of the public transport system (trotro), Kuukua loves to imagine, and writes the stories of the people she meets and interacts with on her daily commute. You can find more of her stories on www.juxkuukuasthoughts.wordpress.com.

Kwabena Agyare Yeboah

Kwabena lives in Accra. He writes poetry, fiction and non-fiction prose.

Kwaku Asiedu Benneh

Kwaku has been writing poems and short stories from an early age. He is currently working on his first book, a collection of short stories, to be published in 2017.

Nana Adwoa Amponsah-Mensah

Nana Adwoa writes as a means of escape. She writes poetry, for the emotional escape, and fiction, to release her wild imagination. She has a blog which focuses mainly on social commentary and random musings on her interactions with her environment. She is a barrister of the Bar of England and Wales.

Nii Moi Thompson

Nii Moi holds degrees in Communication and Air Transport, is an avid writer and reader, and enjoys archaeology and anthropology.

Priscilla Adipa

Priscilla Adipa was born in Accra. Her short stories have been published by Brittle Paper and the Writers' Project of Ghana. Priscilla is currently working on a PhD that examines how art spaces in Accra and Johannesburg attract audiences and facilitate their engagement with art.

Shefi Nelson

Shefi Nelson is an alumna of Ashesi University, who cognizes the power of words and their ability to shape people's perceptions and outlooks on the world. She seeks to make a special contribution to the world by breathing life into words and to have a lasting impact on her readers. Her hobbies include reading, writing and playing tennis.

Connect with
Flash Fiction Ghana Online

Email: flashfictiongh@gmail.com

Twitter: https://twitter.com/FlashFictionGH

Facebook: https://www.facebook.com/FlashFictionGhana